Yosemite Bed and Breakfast

A Novel Set in Yosemite with Lots of Delicious Recipes

Kay Tolladay Pitts

Peregrine Flight

Contents

Cover paintings by Kay Tolladay Pitts
Cover design by Eric Tolladay
Book Production and Publishing Services by Miramare Ponte Press, LLC

Cover design and illustrations by Kay Tolladay Pitts
Hardback ISBN-13: 979-8-9989403-1-6
Paperback ISBN-13:979-8-9989403-0-9
eBook ISBN-13: 979-8-9989403-1-6

Library of Congress Control Number: 2025910028

CHAPTER 1

THE END (ALMOST)

Bad news always seems to come in threes. Disasters, too. When two awful things happen, people brace themselves for the third—for the other shoe to drop. I used to think that was just a silly superstition. I wasn't superstitious. I was an educated woman who relied on facts. That is probably why what happened three years ago hit me extra hard. A bit of belief—something irrational to brace against—might have helped soften the blow.

Three years ago, to the day, my parents died. That same year, I got a divorce. That same season, I began to sense that my job was no longer secure, and I might need to look for a new career. Everything that had once anchored me—my family, my marriage, my profession—collapsed in one sweeping, soul-crushing season.

I wasn't sure how to go forward. It took time, distraction, and more than a few sleepless nights to keep myself from slipping into full-blown depression.

Now, though, I'm a 45-year-old single woman, and I love the independence. I no longer teach, but I'm now running my own business, a Bed and Breakfast in Yosemite National Park called *The Yosemite Butterfly Inn*. That's right. A B&B inside one of the most beautiful places on the planet!

Do I miss teaching? Of course! I loved my job as a choral teacher in the only high school in the small town of Winston, California. But I couldn't stay in the job and survive mentally, so I can accept that it is over. Do I miss my wonderful parents? More than I can ever describe. But, because of their deaths, I inherited a rather run-down property in Yosemite, which I have since upgraded and turned into a thriving business. Do I miss my ex-husband? Not one bit, and when you hear why, you will certainly agree that I am far better off now.

I've been in business for just over a full year, and even though I had to close in August for five days due to forest fires and smoke in the area, and then again last week when the electric company shut off our power for five more days to make repairs, I have still been able to make a small profit and know things will get better.

In hindsight, those hiccups should've prepared me for the odd reservation I received last week. On the reservation form, there is a place to write specific needs, such as food allergies. The woman had written the following note:

Looking forward to staying in your place and meeting my sister after all these years.
Your sister, Evelyn.

When I first read it, I thought she meant she was meeting her sister, whom she hadn't seen for many years, but re-reading it, I realized that it appeared to be addressed to me. Me?

I don't have a sister.

I called my brother, Tommy, and talked about this rather weird note, but he just brushed it off, saying, "She didn't proofread before hitting send. Happens to the best of us."

Chapter 2

Evelyn

She arrived unaccompanied—except for two very large suitcases and a small, yappy dog. Evelyn, not the dog, had a head full of frizzed blonde hair, spike heels, and a bright floral dress that looked pricey. The kind of thing meant for a cocktail party, not a national park.

When I explained that our no-pet policy was clearly stated in the reservation confirmation, I wasn't prepared for her reply.

"I figured that since I'm family, you'd cut me a little slack on the policy. And the rate, too. 'Cause you're really pricey!"

I did my best to hide my confusion, pulling out the smile I reserved for difficult guests. "What exactly do you mean by family?"

"I'm your sister. You ought to be able to tell just by looking at me. We both favor Daddy."

I froze. I'm sure my practiced smile dropped straight into a slack jaw. Total shock and disbelief surged through me, but I forced myself to maintain my cool. If I'd learned anything in my years teaching, it was to never let someone see you rattled. You lose the battle the moment you show surprise or anger.

"Why don't you come upstairs and we can talk over a glass of tea," I said evenly. *Or maybe I'll sneak a glass of brandy for myself.*

We left her luggage in the hallway and stepped onto the deck upstairs to talk. I loved this deck. Deer or coyotes often wandered by on the animal trail below. I was hoping the view would calm me.

Evelyn launched right in, ignoring the scenery as she patted her rat-looking dog.

"Well, Sis, it's like this. Did you ever think of taking one of those DNA tests to find your long-lost relatives?"

My jaw clenched at the forced "Sis," but I managed to answer with restraint. "No, I haven't thought about it."

That wasn't entirely true. I had sent in a DNA sample last year to one of those companies—something to do during the slow season. The results weren't surprising. I was a mix of European ancestry, a genetic mutt.

They offered to reveal "famous" relatives for an additional fee, but it felt like a scam, and even if it wasn't... what would being descended from Henry VIII or Blackbeard really change?

I'd always marveled at groups like the DAR, the Daughters of the American Revolution. Did having a distant ancestor in a centuries-old war somehow make you more dignified?

But more importantly—would it have led me to Evelyn?

"I might have discovered you that way?" I said carefully.

"Too bad you didn't! That's how I found out who my father was. Some relative of yours must've submitted their DNA, and that's how I found you."

She said it like she'd discovered a planet. Galileo with lipstick.

"I didn't know who the man was who used to come to our little house in Merced," she went on. "But I remember that whenever he left, my mother cried. I connected it to money—we didn't have much of it. Mom was a secretary. We lived paycheck to paycheck. Hand-me-downs and Campbell's Soup for dinner. Same Daddy; different lives."

I sat silent. Nothing in my life had prepared me for this kind of shock. I didn't believe her. I couldn't believe my father had ever cheated on my mother. But then that persistent whisper snuck in:

What do you really know about someone else's relationship? Especially your parents'?

4

"Supposing this is true, Evelyn," I said coolly. "I'm not sure why you're here."

I had to stay in control. No flinching. No emotion. Just the composed face of a successful business owner entertaining an unhinged guest.

Evelyn huffed. "Oh, come on, sweetie. You don't look stupid. When I found out that Daddy had died, I did a bit of research. You got this property. Our brother, that hotshot attorney in Washington D.C., got quite a bit of money. So, I'm here for my share! I figure I'll be your business partner, and Bro can just pay me off in cash.

"And then, of course, there's back child support. Mom's gone now, but I think I should be entitled to something for all those years of poverty while your family lived the upper-class life. With interest, that's a tidy pile."

I almost responded to the "upper-class life" bit but caught myself. That would've been a detour. And I needed to stay focused.

"Like I said. Supposing it's true..."

"Of course it's true!" she snapped. "I've got paperwork from my attorney and a photo of our dad with my mom. I'll leave a copy here for you to look at."

She leaned forward, suddenly syrupy. "Having a hard time taking this all in, Sis? It's a lot, I know."

There was a twisted blend of sarcasm and sympathy in her voice. I couldn't even tell which one was real.

"You're wondering how to absorb all this and treat me like your long-lost sister while I'm here for two days," she said. "Don't worry. I don't actually plan to stay. The luggage was just a prop in case we needed more time to chat. But you're a smart cookie. You get it."

"I'm actually heading to Frisco and checking into the JW Marriott. Normally, I stay in dumps, but now that I've found my family and I'm about to get some real money, I figured I'd treat myself."

I said nothing. Sometimes silence is the only defense, especially when you're so stunned you can't trust what might come out of your mouth.

"Come on, Dumpling," she cooed to the dog, scooping him up.

Yes. She actually named him that.

I watched her walk down the stairs, the dog's hair flopping in time with hers. I heard the rumble of her suitcases being wheeled out the front door.

And then, finally, I started to shake. From shock, or relief, or something in between—I wasn't quite sure.

CHAPTER 3

TOMMY

Blindsided by Evelyn, I stumbled out of the house. Her revelations had left me reeling, and if I kept focusing on them, I'd lose it entirely. I had the perfect place to re-center my brain.

My rock.

Since the very first time I saw the house, when our parents bought it, I'd felt a special love for a certain rock. I could hear what my late Irish grandmother would say about "my" rock.

"Are ye daft, girl? You can't own part of nature."

But I did. My rock.

About eight feet tall, flat on top with some nice handholds to help me up, it sat at the edge of the property. Level with the house, it offered a clear view downhill to the west. It's the best place for sunsets, ever.

It was granite, of course. Every rock in Yosemite—be it El Capitan or the ground itself—was granite, shaped by the glaciers of the ice age. Yosemite Valley's glaciers had carved a V-shaped river valley into a U-shaped canyon with cliffs that soar 3,000 feet high. As the glaciers melted, they left huge boulders in some very unexpected areas. In other spots, they polished the granite to a high sheen that could be quite slippery, especially when wet.

Dikes—ribbons of white quartz—ran through at random. Granite often cracked in flat planes, looking for all the world like the leaves of a giant book. Even the dirt you walk on is decomposed granite, and its pale gray color makes it popular for garden paths.

I've always been fascinated by granite. It's especially susceptible to nature's whims: it cracks, it breaks, it forms pockets—just enough for hand and footholds to help me climb.

From the top of My Rock, I had a sweeping, near-360-degree view, or as much as the surrounding forest allowed. Through a break in the trees, I could see sunsets. Below me, an animal trail was visible—and I was not—when a bear, coyote, or deer passed by.

On top, I felt like queen of the mountain.

Years ago, when I first climbed it, I gave myself the name of a famous queen: Guinevere, King Arthur's wife and assumed paramour of Sir Lancelot. Up here, I became her. Queens didn't involve themselves with mere mortal problems. They had to detach from the world in order to solve more universal issues.

And so it had always been for me.

When I was here, much of my world disappeared. The fog in my brain lifted.

And so it went today. When I reached the top, I was immediately calmer. My mind stopped nattering at me. I simply observed.

A squirrel in a nearby sugar pine searched for seeds in the now-ripened cones. He chewed the stem until the cone dropped and seeds sprang free from their hiding place. Most cones hit the soft duff, making little noise. But occasionally, one of those huge twelve-to-eighteen-inch cones would drop on our deck, an unexpected bombing in our peaceful hideaway.

Last spring, I watched a squirrel pick a green cone about nine inches long. He ate it like corn on the cob, rotating it as he chewed in a spiral until he'd tasted every part.

Today, I looked down as a doe appeared on the trail below, followed by a younger one—no doubt her daughter, born this past spring and soon to leave her parent.

My perspective on Evelyn changed as I sat there. At this point, I couldn't do any more about her than I could control the squirrel or the doe.

Until I had input from my brother, I was wasting my time even thinking about her.

Guinevere dismissed this woman from her mind and descended the rock, carefully feeling for footholds.

There was plenty to do in the house: rooms to tidy, reservations to process, the inevitable paperwork any business produces. And when the other guests returned from their afternoon explorations, they'd expect wine, appetizers, and good conversation.

I was grateful for the busyness of my work to distract me from thoughts of Evelyn.

By 6:00, I was the perfect hostess—pleasant and curious about my guests.

"I have a lovely chardonnay tonight, and some grapes, and my homemade CHEDDAR CHIPS," I announced. "These are always popular, and guests almost always ask how they're made. It's an easy recipe to memorize."

I smiled as I recited it:

"Divide 6 oz. (1½ cups) grated cheddar cheese into 12 piles on parchment or nonstick aluminum foil on a baking sheet. Bake them for 18 minutes at 350 degrees. They crisp as they cool. It's about as simple as a recipe can get."

As I served, I asked, "How was your day? Tell me what you liked most about Yosemite Valley."

I tried not to sound like I did this nearly every day. The answers were predictable. Yosemite Falls usually took first place, but this late in the season, when the water became more of a dribble, Half Dome won.

6:45. Time to call Tommy.

I was kicking myself for being so calm when Evelyn made her pronouncement. Why didn't I scream, *"You are a scam artist. None of this is true. Get out of my house. NOW!"*?

Instead, I had focused on staying composed, taking everything in. I let her have the upper hand. She wouldn't have dared to approach Tommy that way. He would've eaten her alive.

Funny thing, genetics. Tommy and I were so different. Not just the boy-girl thing. Tommy started talking when he was eight months old. As our parents used to say, "He has never shut up!"

I was nearly three and still not talking—but I could sing. I couldn't express myself very well until kindergarten, and even then, not so much. But I could remember lyrics. I still can.

My head is full of songs from all kinds of genres, crowding out far more important stuff.

Hoping he hadn't gone to bed yet—and cursing the rotating planet that made time zones a thing—I made the call.

He picked up. He didn't sound sleepy.

As I recounted Evelyn's visit, he stayed calm. I sometimes forgot how well trial attorneys learned to keep their emotions in check.

When I finally finished, he said, "Do you remember when we were kids, how shocked we were to realize we were born because our parents had had sex?

"This feels like that. It's just as hard, as an adult, to think a parent might have had an affair. But it happens.

"Scan and send me everything she gave you—the paperwork from her attorney, the photo, anything else. I smell a scam. But I'm baffled about the DNA. I can't believe this about our dad, either. But until I see her so-called evidence, I can't do anything."

His practicality was in direct contrast to my raving.

As I scanned and sent the documents, I kept ranting. "Look at the photo! That has to be Dad. With her mom."

"Moni, honey, calm down," he said. "I see a blurry photo of a tall man with a short woman. From the clothes, maybe the '80s. It could be Dad. It could be almost any tall man. And there's no proof that the woman is her mother. There's so much information online now. People seem desperate to share their lives with the world. Maybe one of our cousins posted an old photo of Dad with a neighbor. We just don't know yet. Let me go through everything. I'll call you back tomorrow night. Okay?"

"You should've seen this bitch, Tommy. She can't be our dad's child. She can't be related to us. She's going after your money—but she's trying to ruin my life! Everything I've worked for these past three years could be destroyed. If this is somehow true, I'd have to leave my business. My home. There's no way I could work with her as a partner. It's got to be a scam."

"Yeah," he said quietly. "And it could be a very expensive one to prove."

And that's what terrified me most.

CHAPTER 4

PARENTS' DEATH

I went to bed, but my head was too full to sleep. I lay there restless, my thoughts dragging me backward to three years ago today—the day my parents died.

They were driving from Fresno on Highway 41, that winding two-lane road that leads to Yosemite, when, it is supposed, Daddy had a heart attack on one of the more treacherous turns. Or perhaps he was just momentarily blinded by the setting sun or distracted by his usual monologue when they traveled.

Daddy was still a good-looking man, his upright posture and obvious fitness betraying his military background as a pilot in Vietnam and continuing presence in the National Guard, where he was a colonel. He was past the age of military retirement, but he continued to volunteer—a true patriot. His dark hair had faded to a steel gray, always kept short. His skin was weathered and clearly showed his age of 78 years.

Mom, on the other hand, seemed ageless. Her skin, for a woman of 75, was still fairly smooth, kept that way by her habit of always wearing a hat in the sun. Her short, ash-colored hair had light highlights by way of a hairdresser—not nature's bounty—but a casual look assumed it to be natural. She had an air of innocence, of naiveté, that was truly her and not some attempt to remain girlish.

Age hadn't dulled her brain. She had been practicing medicine in some of the rural, underserved areas of the Central Valley until two years prior.

Post-military retirement, Dad had gone into business—mostly to keep himself busy—and done quite well for himself. Now in his second retirement, he sometimes accompanied Mom on her rounds of small towns and farms, her standby nurse, taking orders from her easily and never betraying displeasure in this somewhat subservient position.

"Marge, when we get to the house, remind me to check the generator and the pipe from the propane tank. And let's make a list of the things we need to shop for when we'…"

On and on went his usual monologue.

Mother was probably dozing, as she often did, to ease the nausea of the curves—or to tune him out entirely. After 44 years of marriage, she could probably recite the conversation before they even left Fresno.

A fire had swept the hills the summer before, and the natural vegetation had been reduced to ash. A freak summer storm had brought mudslides. While they seldom blocked the road, they could leave it very slick.

Driving into the sun as evening approached, the sheen of dark mud may not be noticed until you are in it—and could whip your car sideways before you knew what happened.

If you're lucky, it would whip you toward the mountain, where you might get a crumpled fender and the scare of your life. This had happened to me once, and I can guarantee it made me a more cautious driver.

I was pretty sure there was no heart attack in Dad's case. Just the mud slick.

Maybe Daddy had been cautious. Maybe he'd tried to correct the slide. Maybe Mom woke up and reached for the wheel too late.

But I chose to believe she was asleep—that she never knew what happened.

And I clung to the hope that it had been his heart after all, that he didn't spend his final moments knowing he'd taken her with him.

Of course, I'd never really know. There was little point in speculating. They were both gone. The best I could do through my grief was hold to the fact that they died together. That felt right. The proper end to their really wonderful marriage.

And then the niggling doubt again: Was their wonderful marriage all a sham?

As I drifted off, I asked myself, *How could Evelyn have a photo of my dad with her mother? Who would have taken the photo?* Evelyn would've been too young to hold the camera steady enough.

In the days before smartphones, a "selfie" required that a camera be mounted on a tripod or a secure surface. Aim carefully, set the timer, and run back to your spot, then say, "Cheese."

If they were so poor that they were eating Campbell's soup for dinner, how could they afford the camera?

Maybe the man brought it.

But if he were carrying on an illicit affair, it seems curious that he would take photos.

With today's technology, probably any photo could be manipulated. And with today's technology, so could faces be reborn. For all I knew, Evelyn could be ten years older than she looked. Could she even be older than me?

It's curious that her visit coincided with the anniversary of my parents' deaths.

Or did she plan it that way?

She might be an even bigger bitch than I'd first thought. And far more dangerous than Tommy realized.

Chapter 5

Looking Back

The next day was one of the hardest I had ever faced—making breakfast, smiling and chatting with the guests, and pretending my life wasn't quietly imploding.

I made a "blindfold breakfast," one of those reliable recipes I could do with my eyes closed. That morning, a simple breakfast of fruit, muffins from the freezer, and a SPINACH AND MUSHROOM FRITTATA.

Frittatas are really simple and can be made with almost any combination of vegetables. I sautéed some mushrooms in olive oil and added half a bag of organic spinach, covering it for three minutes or so to let the spinach wilt.

While I waited, I beat six eggs, adding the juice of one lemon, and a dash of salt.

Lemon is my secret ingredient—it adds lightness and replaces some of the salt that eggs require.

I poured the eggs over the veggies, covered the pan, and turned the heat to low for about fifteen minutes. When the eggs had partially set, I sprinkled some grated cheese on top with some freshly ground black pepper.

I cut it into four slices and served it with a side of fresh fruit and an assortment of muffins.

I probably should have cooked up some bacon, but bacon requires attention while on the stove, and I was too scattered and shattered for that.

Instead, I quickly fried up some leftover ham slices from a ham I had bought for a community picnic. I always bought a ham with a bone, as once the meat is pretty much used up, what remains on the bone is perfect for a potato dumpling dish, supposedly of Norwegian origin, called KUMLA. That in turn becomes the basis for SPLIT PEA SOUP.

But none of that mattered right then. I needed to be outside. I needed to breathe the mountain air.

I took a short walk to the community mailboxes, and on my return, paused in front of my home—my business—and let myself feel it. The memories flooded in.

I'd been thirteen in 1986 when my parents bought the house. It was already ten years old and hadn't been well-maintained.

A modest three-bedroom bungalow, about 1,500 square feet, built on a slope that led down to a creek.

The community, Yosemite West, consisted of several acres of private land that the Park nearly surrounded as its boundaries expanded over the years.

You could only reach it by going through the park's entrance gate. Still, it wasn't technically in the park.

As a teen, I didn't pay attention to our vacation home. It was simply home base for my hiking, exploring, and skiing. While my folks, my brother, and I did explore all areas of Yosemite, most of my explorations in those first years before I could drive were spent exploring the area of Yosemite West.

"Don't go out alone without Bingo," Mom would always say.

"And stay on the trails," they'd both warn. "Watch out for bears and mountain lions."

Of course, I didn't listen.

Bingo, our impressive 90-pound German shepherd, was off-leash the moment we were out of sight.

I certainly wasn't worried about bears. After all, I was thirteen and immortal. Black bears are much shyer around people and they are seldom actually black in color. Usually, they were more chocolate or cinnamon. They are great seekers of free food and have the proper noses to get them to a source.

What they were, though, was persistent—and their noses could sniff out a snack from a mile away.

You have to be very careful about leaving food in your car. Tourists who don't read the warnings often return to their cars from a short walk to find that a bear broke in for an empty soda can left under the seat or the mints in the glove compartment.

The professional bears shatter the glass and clear the frame before climbing through. The amateurs skip that step and just rip off the car door entirely.

When I was first married and Julie was small, it became less the place to hike, more the place we visited on holidays. Christmas was always particularly magical.

Most kids who grow up in California are a bit confused by the Christmas cards, the children's books, and the TV shows all depicting scenes of snow and sleighs, happy families gathered around a cozy fireplace, icicles at the window and snowflakes drifting down.

Not in California.

It can get cold, but rather laughable by East Coast standards. Even nights are seldom below freezing.

That's why our cabin was so magical in winter. The Sierra Nevada mountains do get snow. Lots of snow! So much snow that when it melts in the spring, it feeds down to the Central Valley, keeping cities and crops alive the rest of the year.

Sometimes we'd arrive, cars stuffed with presents and holiday food, only to spend the first hour digging out the driveway from six feet of snow.

Once our parents retired and lived there full time, they, with the help of a snowplow, could usually keep up with the increasing snowpack.

And we would have a week of magic: a beautiful tree with the ornaments we had so carefully crafted over the years, slide shows of Christmases past, and eggnogs, which Tommy and I had become adept at sneaking a bit of rum into long before we were legal; skiing and hiking were replaced with snow angels, sledding, and snowball fights.

Everything you don't get in most of the state.

After my parents' memorial, with wonderful memories running through my mind, I had driven up alone just to be, once again, on my rock. I needed to refocus on my inheritance. I was now a property owner!

The house was definitely showing its age. I wondered when the roof had started shedding shingles or when the front door began to sag. If houses have personality, this one said, "I'm really tired."

The four small windows, made even smaller with their four-inch square panes, flanked the front door, which faced the street. Even on the creek side, where the views were really nice, the windows were small and again broken up by small panes.

I had hated those windows.

When my brother or I committed some infraction of the family rules, we had to wash those little windows as punishment.

I can still hear my dad's voice, "Young lady, you aren't showing much respect for your parents or this property. See what you can do with twelve windowpanes."

I knew, at the time, that no matter what I decided to do with the house, those windows would be history.

I took lots of photos, measured the rooms, and made a floor plan. I had several options when it first became mine: sell it, keep it as a family vacation retreat, repair it and turn it into a vacation rental.

Maybe tear it down and start over?

I didn't like any of the options. I needed help. Fortunately, I knew I could depend on my husband, Jack, who had a really good, no-nonsense way of viewing the world.

I drove back home to Winston, our small town south of Fresno.

At least... I thought I could.

The front door slammed, jarring me out of the memory.

I turned to see guests, a retired couple from Ohio and a young pair from L.A., heading out for an afternoon hike.

I waved goodbye and offered my usual warning about bears and mountain lions.

As I turned back toward the house, I thought again about Jack—his good, no-nonsense worldview.

And how grateful I was to be rid of him.

CHAPTER 6

HELP FROM JACK

Jack had been a physician's assistant, a PA, but six years earlier, he left the hospital and opened a weight loss clinic. The business took off quickly.

Most of the clients were women—struggling with overeating, poor food choices, and a lack of exercise. They needed a sympathetic ear, and my handsome husband, with his charming smile and soft-spoken nature, was the perfect man to confide in.

One afternoon, I got home around 3:00 p.m. and called him to see when he might be home. He had another "late night," but promised to be home by seven for dinner.

With time on my hands, I decided to get ahead on bills. The hotel charge from a recent San Francisco conference in late August seemed unusually high.

I recalled our conversation before he left for that trip. "Honey, I've got another conference in San Francisco next week. Sorry, you can't go this time—mid-week instead of a weekend."

"Me too. Unfortunately, I start back to school that week. Don't fall off the cable car and watch out for female predators. You're pretty cute! Is the conference at the Hyatt again?"

"Yeah."

"Remember that amazing room we had the last time we were there? The one where our neighbors were complaining because we were making too much noise in bed!"

We both laughed at that memory of great sex after so many years of marriage.

I knew he would at least save money and book a single room. That's why I was quite surprised to see the charge. The charge was for a double room.

I called the Hyatt to confirm the conference rate.

"Yes, Mrs. Gilroy, we did set a single rate, but you reserved a double room."

"There's got to be a mistake—" I started.

"Actually, I'm glad you called," the receptionist continued. "Your husband left behind a tie—the one that perfectly matched your scarf when you both checked in. It went so beautifully with your red hair. We tried to contact him but haven't heard back. It's waiting here at the front desk if you'd like to let him know."

"Thank you," I replied, as evenly as I could manage. "I'll pass that on."

I hung up the phone and sat frozen.

I didn't go with Jack.

And I am not a redhead.

My head was full of scrambled eggs, left too long in the pan—greasy and overcooked. I sat very, very still for an hour and then poured myself a shot of vodka. This was Jack's late night at the clinic.

Or was it?

It had never occurred to me to check on him. Now I began to wonder. Were the once-a-week late nights real? Who was he seeing? For how long? Was he in love? Were there others? How could he do this to me?

I considered pouring another vodka. Maybe just a glass of wine. I was losing my mind—and control of it.

What do I say? What should I say? What can I possibly say?

I'm in love with this man! I don't want my marriage to end. I want to start the world over. I want my mommy.

Jack came home, of course; a scene—a fight born of alcohol, rage on my part, and guilt on his.

By the time he got home, I had morphed into Hercule Poirot, connecting dots I had ignored for far too long. But the truth was always there—I had just refused to see it.

And then there was Giselle.

My best friend.

Giselle was a fashion consultant who sometimes traveled for work. Tall, stunning, always perfectly dressed, and yes—red-haired.

We had been sorority sisters at U.C. Berkeley and she had remained in the Bay Area when I moved to Winston. But rising housing prices convinced her to move and since she did much of her work online, she decided to move to Winston as well.

A home here was half the price it would be in San Francisco.

Over the years, whenever Jack had to go out of town, Giselle and I would have a girls' night out. But this past year or so, our tradition had faded, as her shows somehow coincided with Jack's business meetings.

My best friend.

What a joke.

CHAPTER 7

DIVORCE

Jack and I separated and filed for divorce.

Every day, I went to school hoping that teaching would reclaim its rightful place in my mind—the dominant force that pushed everything else aside when I stepped into the classroom.

Instead, death and divorce had hard coded themselves into my brain, always humming in the background, always ready to hijack my focus. I needed another outlet.

I tried wine, but after a few nights of downing a bottle and trying to teach the next day with a hangover, I realized I wasn't cut out for alcoholism.

I tried a trial membership at a gym, working out my anger on the machines, though in hindsight, I should have tried boxing.

I was on the treadmill one day when the woman next to me started a conversation. Talking while speed-walking wasn't easy, so we decided to go out for coffee and get better acquainted. Her name was Rosella, and we seemed to be around the same age.

As we sipped our coffee, we discovered we had similar backgrounds, including husbands who couldn't keep their pants zipped.

Our conversation that day was rather brief, as we each had commitments, but we agreed to meet the following week.

That's when we got to the down and dirty.

"Men are awful!"

"All of them are pigs!"

"Women should run the world!"

We were on a roll. It was exhilarating to let it all vent. She told me about the affair, about the betrayal, about how long she'd been in denial.

I told her how my husband wouldn't help with Julie or the chores. Sometimes he would stop speaking to me for days, and I wouldn't know why.

Once, when I had made his favorite dessert, BERRY AND CREAM PIE, he said he didn't want any. The reason?

He had found bath towels left in the dryer and wondered just what I was doing in all my "spare time."

We tried counseling, and he agreed to end the affair and do more to help around the house.

The next day, I asked him to make the orange juice; I didn't want to overwhelm him. I had put the thawed can by a pitcher, figuring he could read the directions.

Instead, he decided to relax in the recliner and read the paper.

When I asked why he wasn't making the orange juice, he replied, "You didn't say please!"

So, I did say, "Please."

I said, "Please get out of this house. NOW."

Until Rosella, I hadn't told anyone the full story. Saying it aloud was strangely healing. And surprisingly fun.

She didn't judge me—she got it. I felt like we were soul sisters.

Here's what happened to the pie. I tossed it across the room and went for a long walk. I didn't, EVER, make that pie again.

But you should. It's extremely easy and absolutely delicious.

BERRY AND CREAM PIE

You will need a piecrust, either homemade or purchased.

Put it in your 9" pie tin and fill with 1 quart of washed berries.

Boysenberries are best but you can use any mixture of fresh berries.

You can use frozen berries in the off-season but you'll need to add an extra tablespoon of flour to the sugar.

Pour the following over the berries:

- 1 cup sugar mixed with 1/4 cup flour and 1 teaspoon cinnamon
- To this, stir in 1 cup whipping cream
- Bake at 400–425°F for 45 minutes.
- Don't throw it across the room. It makes an awful mess.

I admired Rosella a lot. Her body was quite sculpted and she looked really great for a woman of 45. Her only imperfection was a deeply lined face, which made her appear several years older.

As we chatted, she asked how long I had been divorced.

"We've just been separated two months now but the divorce will be final in four more. How about you?"

"It's been 5 years."

I got home and looked in the mirror. I realized that I could store all that bitterness and my face could look like Rosella's.

Or I could take my brain back and get on with my life.

CHAPTER 8

EVELYN AGAIN

It was time to get my head back to the present.

The guests had checked out, which meant I had two rooms to clean. Fortunately, no one new was arriving that day, which gave me time to catch up on my neglected paperwork. Despite the persistent reminders from my accountant, it remained the only part of running a business that I truly disliked.

As I sat at my desk, dithering, the phone rang—a welcome interruption that brought a brief, inexplicable jolt of joy. The call was from Lori, my art teacher friend from Winston High.

Lori and I had made plans to visit the east side of the Sierras in October to see the quaking aspen when the leaves change from green to more shades of gold than you knew existed.

I figured that was why she was calling, but Lori never eased into things. "I was just checking the reviews of your business on Skweel," she said, "and there's a really awful one posted yesterday."

As I opened my browser to find the site, she read it to me:

"I had the most awful experience at the Yosemite Butterfly Inn. The owner greeted me sullenly and when I was shown to my room, I made a brief inspection and found the linens hadn't been changed nor did it appear the room had even been cleaned. When I complained to the owner, she became even ruder, and when I demanded my money back, she curtly refused a refund. I can't imagine why anyone would choose to stay there!"

Evelyn. Of course.

I gave Lori a brief rundown of my past two days and promised to completely fill her in during our trip. I thanked her for the heads up and hung up, trying to steady my breathing. Evelyn probably had the review written before she even arrived.

Skweel was one of several travel and lodging review sites, but unlike most, it seemed to encourage negative reviews, snark, and negativity. A play on "squeal," the site practically invited people to air grievances, which often border on nasty.

Luckily, my reviews were almost always glowing, so I hoped this one wouldn't do too much damage.

I had one previous review on Skweel. At the time I called the company, pointing out the impossibility of the date, and threatened to sue for defamation unless it was taken down.

I figured the review had been posted by some teens having their idea of fun, possibly former students. They complied—but grudgingly.

Since then, they require that submitters verify their stay. Unfortunately, Evelyn had a reservation, and I was stuck with her lie. How many other ways would she try to sabotage me?

I hoped Tommy had found time to dig through the materials I sent him and would call with some clarity that evening.

My conversation with Tommy wasn't encouraging.

I guess I expected to be rescued, but as he put it:

"I'm here in Washington and I don't know the first thing about DNA testing or how Evelyn could have so-called proof she's our sister. I think you might consider hiring a private detective to investigate the situation. It's only fair I cover the costs, since you'll have to do the legwork."

He was right. But I was overwhelmed. This whole situation was becoming messier by the day.

Reluctantly, I researched detective agencies online. There were three in Merced and several in Fresno. I decided to go with one in Fresno—it was closer, and more importantly, since Evelyn claimed to be from Merced, I didn't want to hire someone who might possibly know her. I called around, looking for someone who had at least a basic understanding of genealogy and ancestry cases.

I arranged for an appointment the next day with Jonathan Steele. How could I resist a name like that?

But when I walked into his office the next day, I almost turned around. Paperwork was scattered across every surface—floor, desk, chairs—and he looked like a walking afterthought: rumpled clothes and a face in need of a shave. So much for the rugged private eye I'd imagined.

Perhaps his parents were very hopeful for their son's future—or maybe he'd renamed himself for marketing. Either way, it had worked. It got me through the door.

"Sorry for all of this," he said, gesturing vaguely around the office. "I unexpectedly had to go undercover yesterday and spent the night out. I really do clean up pretty good!"

I'm sure my face betrayed my hesitation, but I gave a polite, "It's okay," even though it wasn't.

But if I looked beyond the mess and the stubble, I could see a pleasant-looking man in his late forties.

He had no really distinguishing characteristics: medium height, maybe 5'10," nondescript brown hair just longer than the current fashion, hazel eyes, and weathered skin.

A guy who could easily get lost in a crowd. A guy you would never remember. Which, I supposed, was exactly what made him good at his job. I set aside my disappointment that he wasn't James Bond and explained the Evelyn situation from the beginning.

His response wasn't reassuring.

"While it sounds fraudulent, you have to be prepared to face the possibility that she is telling the truth, that your dad was unfaithful. I have done some work of this kind, and I am pretty sure I can find out if she's legitimate or a con artist. It will take a while, and I will have to travel to Merced and possibly other places."

We discussed his stiff fees, but since my brother was paying, so it goes!

"Out of curiosity," he asked, "how did you decide to open a bed and breakfast?"

"Well, how much time do you have?" I asked half-jokingly.

CHAPTER 9

WHAT TO DO

I was still reeling a bit from the divorce when I knew it was time to focus on the Yosemite property.

It was mid-October, and the dogwood leaves were shifting into their autumn palette—rich reds and burgundies fluttering to the ground—while the oaks took up the slack, turning to rich golds and russets.

Julie came with me on this trip to the house. Julie was a sophomore at California State University, Fresno, locally known as Fresno State. She had inherited her father's coloring: dark hair, pale skin, and those piercing azure eyes. She stood several inches taller than me, with a slender, athletic build and a maturity far beyond her years.

Even from a young age, she'd been intentional—always setting goals and considering how her choices would affect others. She had been nothing short of extraordinary through the trauma of the divorce, giving me good counsel without choosing sides.

Every time I thought about throwing a pity party for myself over the philandering husband, I realized it would be a solo act; I would get no support from Julie. Julie wasn't going to join me in my misery.

So, even though the marriage ended, Jack and I had created something beautiful together. If you'll pardon the pun, she's a true jewel.

When we arrived at the house, Julie and I did a full walk-through, as if we were real estate agents evaluating a listing. We agreed not to let our nostalgia for past holidays and family warmth cloud our judgment as we evaluated the property.

The three small bedrooms and one bathroom looked dingy and worn. I couldn't believe we ever survived with just one bathroom. The kitchen was worn and outdated, the appliances ancient. The dining table and chairs were losing essential parts, and sitting down felt like a gamble. The sofa sagged and the fireplace hadn't been used in years.

"Mom! Those windows have to go!" Julie exclaimed.

Already decided.

It was a discouraging tour. Everything needed attention.

"Maybe we should just sell it," I sighed.

"No way, Mom! I love this place."

We walked through again but only got more discouraged. I didn't want to sell either, but even with some money coming from the divorce settlement, I had no idea how much a full renovation might cost. And once it was fixed, would we even use it enough to justify the expense? There seemed to be no good answers.

Renting it out seemed like the most logical solution—but even then, it would need to be in better shape. And did I really want strangers staying in my home?

"Let's drive down to Yosemite Valley and take a short hike. Maybe we'll get some inspiration," Julie suggested.

I loved how she was helping me, gently nudging me out of my funk. I'm sure she thought this project might be the thing to pull me forward.

We decided to take a loop trail to Mirror Lake, starting and ending at the famous Ahwahnee Hotel.

Though there was space in the small parking lot, we decided to pretend we were arriving movie stars and drove under the wide portico to have valet parking. The pretense was shattered almost immediately as the attendant recognized me.

"Hi, Mrs. Gilroy. Here for lunch today?"

So much for passing as movie stars—but still, it felt nice to be recognized as a local. Of course, I still had to tip him, even though he probably made double my income. But sometimes you just have to lean into the fantasy.

We walked down the red carpet and approached the entry.

"Eyes straight ahead, Mom. Do not—I repeat, do not—look to the right. Ignore the gift shop."

She knew how easily I could be tempted by the beautiful scarves, gorgeous glassware, Ahwahnee plates, and Yosemite books. We bypassed the overpriced enticements, but just barely.

"Just think, Mom," she said, "Maybe once we fix up the house, we'll need some of these glorious goodies for the décor!"

The whole hotel, both inside and out, was grand and timeless, almost impossible to describe adequately. Like Yosemite, you run out of adjectives when you try to describe it. The entrance—imposing. The view—breathtaking. The wooden beams—fake. Those beams and pillars were made of concrete, designed to look like wood.

Stephen Mather, the first director of the Park Service, wanted a magnificent hotel to grace the magnificent Valley, but he feared fire. So, he wisely insisted on fireproof materials—concrete and stone.

The lobby was impressive with its thick columns and views to the patio and lawn areas.

The check-in desk was quite busy with people willing to spend upward of $500 for a room here.

We wandered past the desk to the hall with its paintings by Thomas Hill, past the fireplace and the beautiful floral arrangement on the nearby table, to peek into the dining room. It was a huge, inspiring room with its high ceilings. Its tall windows overlooked Half Dome and Glacier Point, and an alcove that framed a perfect view of Yosemite Falls.

The food was pricey but nearly always perfect. My folks splurged a few times a year for Sunday brunch here.

And twice—only twice—we attended the Bracebridge Dinner. That experience stayed with me.

We continued our tour through the Great Lounge—towering ceilings, oversized chairs, and fireplaces that encouraged lingering. We ducked into the Winter Club Room to admire the old ski photos, which gave a good history of snow activities in Yosemite, most from Badger Pass, the nearby ski area. I've often thought that if I ever retire, I'd love to teach skiing there.

We exited through the Sun Room, the half-circle living room at the hotel's south end, with postcard views of Half Dome and Glacier Point.

Above us was the Kennedy Suite, named for the assassinated president. You could rent the living room and the suite with its balcony for a king's ransom. I'd always thought it the best spot to watch summer hang gliders leap off Glacier Point and float down to the Valley floor.

Crossing the lawn, we enjoyed the dogwood trees, like those in front of the hotel, their leaves bursting in fall color—golds, pinks, reds, and burgundies. We picked up the bike path, crossed the Merced River, and followed the mostly flat route to Mirror Lake.

Mirror Lake was more pond than lake—a calm, wide spot in Tenaya Creek with a perfect reflection of Half Dome above. Even with the crowds and the click of cameras, the scene never lost its magic.

We took pictures like we always did, even though we knew they'd never quite capture the moment. We returned along the narrow trail hugging the cliff, past piles of rockfall, eventually looping back to the Ahwahnee. Still, as we drove home, inspiration hadn't struck. Maybe food would help.

We made our favorite dessert—PEACH COBBLER—hoping for an epiphany. But aside from the deliciousness of the cobbler, we came up empty.

My friend, Lori, asked: "Have you thought about turning it into a bed and breakfast? A friend of mine stayed in one and really liked it. It was somewhere on the East Coast and George Washington had slept there—or maybe it was someone else. But I know it was someone historical."

I laughed. On the East Coast, history drips from every brick. But Yosemite certainly has history too, and definitely name recognition.

Maybe Lori was on to something.

I did some online checking, and while I didn't see any bed and breakfasts in Yosemite, I noticed something: Every place within fifty miles used "Yosemite" in their name.

My advantage? My house was actually *inside* the park gates.

CHAPTER 10

TOURING B&BS

The bed and breakfast idea had taken root. I liked to cook, I didn't mind cleaning, and I knew enough about bookkeeping to manage the numbers. And every morning, I could wake the guests with a song—okay, maybe not. But the idea intrigued me. The main drawback was that I already had a career I loved—teaching. And while the year hadn't started well under our new principal, I'd weathered other incompetents before, and I figured I could weather this one, too.

Still, I had nearly three months off in the summer, the height of Yosemite's tourist season. Maybe I could open the place just for that stretch and keep teaching the rest of the year.

Since I knew absolutely nothing about running a bed and breakfast, I started asking around. None of my colleagues had ever stayed in one, which surprised me. So, I turned to the Internet and quickly discovered there were more B&Bs in California than I'd imagined. It seemed like a good idea to visit a few before diving in. I was sure Julie would be on board.

"Julie," I said, "instead of coming up here for Thanksgiving, I have a better idea."

"Sure, Mom. I'm always up for better! So, what's better going to be?"

"Lori suggested I turn the Yosemite property into a bed and breakfast. Since I've never even stayed in one, I thought we could visit a couple—get a feel for them."

"I think Lori might be onto something," she said. "Let's go exploring. Besides, you haven't exactly loved your teaching job this year with your new principal, so maybe it's time to think about a career change."

I booked us into two different inns in the foothills near Yosemite for the Thanksgiving break.

The first one billed itself as a "cozy cottage." It was a faux Craftsman, probably built in the 1930s, and had clearly been refurbished more than once. There were only two guest rooms and a shared bathroom between them. At first, we liked the idea of a shared bath—until we actually tried to use it.

We turned in around 9 p.m., since there wasn't much going on in the small town. After reading for a bit, we got ready for bed—except the bathroom was occupied. It stayed occupied. How many people were in that other room? Were they all taking back-to-back showers? By the time I finally got in, nearly two hours later, I was about to burst. Poor Julie! She let me go first, probably assuming my bladder had more urgency than hers.

By the time we were both ready for bed, it was after eleven, and sleep was hard to come by. When I woke up at 2:00 a.m. needing to pee again, you guessed it—the bathroom was busy. That was the last straw. If I ever opened a bed and breakfast, every room would have its own bathroom.

The second inn was a complete contrast, very upscale in both decor and pricing. Our room felt like a luxury suite. The sheets were the softest I'd ever slept between, the bathroom was modern, and the shower had more spray settings than I knew what to do with. For an extra $60, we could have had a Jacuzzi tub. Breakfast was brought to our room, and we could eat in bed or out on the private terrace. It was clearly designed for romance, which we weren't exactly in the mood for, being mother and daughter.

The food, though, was fantastic, especially the ROSE EGGS, which I just had to learn how to make. I managed to squeeze the recipe out of the unsuspecting breakfast courier, who also worked in the kitchen. She told me the trick was to grease muffin tins and line them with thin slices of Black Forest ham—the petals of the rose. A few sautéed mushrooms went in the bottom, then a cracked egg on top, and finally a tablespoon of sour cream. They baked them at 350 degrees for 15 minutes, just until the egg whites were set.

They served two of those eggs alongside blueberry muffins and fresh fruit. It was delicious, but the experience still felt impersonal. We didn't meet a single other guest. We might as well have been at a fancy hotel.

Still, that host mentioned CABBI—the California Association of Bed and Breakfast Inns. She said she'd learned a lot through one of their seminars. I looked it up on my laptop and saw they were offering a three-day class in Santa Barbara right after Christmas: So You Want to Be an Innkeeper. I called and managed to grab the last available spot.

The class was eye-opening—both informative and, admittedly, a little discouraging. For starters, the average burnout rate for innkeepers was three years. That gave me pause. It suggested the business could be more exhausting than I'd imagined.

Another issue was profitability. We were told you needed at least five rooms to make a good living from it, and I could only have three. Not just because of my budget, but due to a county ordinance that capped rentals at three guest rooms. Still, I learned a lot—how to manage guests, how to market, how to streamline daily operations. Each instructor had real-world experience and practical advice.

Our small group of six stayed in three different inns during the course. The first inn had a shared bathroom, reinforcing everything I had already learned the hard way. The second inn was the most practical in layout and had an architectural style that gave me ideas for my own space. The third inn served the best breakfast of them all—so good it made your mouth water before you even took a bite.

That innkeeper also gave us a surprise cooking class. "Today," she said, "we're serving a special recipe we created here at our inn: YIN-YANG MELON SOUP. We don't usually share our secrets—but this one's just too fun not to teach."

We filed into the kitchen where six wide, white soup bowls waited for us.

"In the blenders," she explained, "we have two melon soups— cantaloupe in one, honeydew in the other. We've also folded strips of aluminum foil into an 'S' shape and placed them in the center of each bowl."

Another single lady and I were chosen as the first potential victims for ruining breakfast. She held the foil while I poured the cantaloupe soup on one side and honeydew on the other—carefully, simultaneously, and then she removed the foil.

And there it was—a perfect orange and green yin-yang symbol in the bowl. We finished our second bowl, then each placed two blueberries in the "eyes" of the symbol.

Simple. Elegant. And surprisingly achievable. Just like the dream that was starting to form.

CHAPTER 11

ROACH

Though I usually looked forward to returning to teaching after Christmas break, this year felt different. With everything that had happened—the deaths of my parents, the divorce—I had managed to temporarily forget the third major upheaval in my life: the new principal at our high school.

For five wonderful years, Samantha had been our principal. She was fair with students, incredibly supportive of the staff, and someone I genuinely admired. When she left suddenly last September, the rumor mill kicked into high gear.

"She had an affair with a teacher."

"No, it was with a student."

"No, her husband had the affair!"

Everyone seemed to *know* something, swearing they had witnessed some sort of scandal. In the end, the truth was far less salacious: Her husband had received a major promotion that required relocating to Paris. Who could blame her for going? She took a year's leave of absence that soon became permanent, and we were left to adjust to her replacement.

Enter Harold Jackson Roachmire. "Call me Hal," he told us, all rah-rah smiles and empty promises. He had a vision: Winston High would become the best school in the city, the county, maybe even the state. Our football team would be the stuff of legends. Our debate team? Unbeatable. Our art students would take top honors, and the music department—my department—would be second to none.

To his face, we called him Hal. Behind his back, however, most of the staff referred to him simply as *Roach*, or occasionally something more creative that played on his unfortunate middle name.

The trouble started at the very first faculty meeting of the year. We had a long-standing tradition of bringing snacks to our twice-monthly meetings—homemade treats, store-bought goodies, and always coffee. It was my turn, and I had baked a batch of my well-loved PECAN PIE MUFFINS, which are more cookie than muffin, really. I proudly placed them on the table and got the coffee brewing.

Roach looked genuinely startled.

"You all realize I consider this a professional business meeting," he said, glancing at the spread with obvious disapproval. "This isn't a coffee klatch. No snacks or coffee during meetings moving forward. That's not how real corporations operate."

That was our first clue.

I had a one-on-one meeting with him soon after—his "Let's Get Acquainted" session, which quickly turned into a thinly veiled critique of my teaching record.

"Really, Mrs. Gilroy, don't you think there's room for improvement?" he asked, flipping through my file as if reading the stats of a second-string quarterback.

I calmly explained that unlike schools with a robust music program, Winston's feeder schools had no choir in elementary or middle school. Most of my students had never read music before and didn't know a whole note from a half note. My job was 90% foundational training, something they should have received long before high school.

"I don't like excuses. I like action," he said with his trademark chirpiness, giving my shoulder a patronizing little pat. "From now on, Winston stands for WIN."

Actually, I thought, it stood for *wince*—every time he opened his mouth.

Lori and I, along with a few other teachers, started meeting after school just to vent. We called it "staff therapy." Roach had been a football coach before ascending to his imagined pedestal of academic leadership, and he treated every teacher like we were fumbling JV players. Those of us in the arts—music, visual arts, drama—fields he clearly didn't understand, were hit the hardest by his micromanagement.

And while I still loved my students and the core of what I did, the mental and emotional toll of working under someone so disconnected from the classroom was wearing me down. I started to think maybe Julie was right. Maybe it really *was* time for a career change.

CHAPTER 12

BACK TO SCHOOL

I wavered constantly between my options. On paper, it seemed insane to leave a perfectly good job, one I generally liked, to start a business I knew almost nothing about. But the idea wouldn't leave me alone. I thought a lot about my teaching job, which I'd been doing for twenty years. I was the only choral music teacher at the school, which meant I taught everyone, from absolute beginners to the advanced mixed choir. Over the years, my groups entered festivals and competitions regularly. We always placed well, and sometimes, we even won top honors.

But I shouldn't have been surprised that Roach didn't see my work the same way. He called me into his office not long after the December county-wide competition. Out of thirty schools, we had placed quite respectably, and I was proud of the kids. Roach, however, saw it differently. I sat across from him as he launched into one of his classic lectures.

"Winston means WIN," he snapped, stabbing the air with his finger. "And I'm talking to *you*. I want a first-place finish at the next competition."

I explained—again—that we had no feeder music program. My students came to me with no background. I was essentially building a music foundation from scratch, turning "raw recruits" into a cohesive choir. I even leaned into a metaphor I thought might resonate with him.

"They're like Marines," I said. "Only they skipped basic training. I'm building them from the ground up."

Given that Roach had been a Marine colonel, I thought maybe—*maybe*—he'd get it.

He did not.

In fact, he turned crimson, and I could actually see a vein pulsing in his forehead. He stood up so fast his chair slammed into the wall behind him.

"Don't give me your crappy excuses!" he screamed, spittle flying. "You are to win... *or else!*"

He looked completely unhinged. For a terrifying second, I thought he might have a heart attack right there. And if I'm being honest, I was kind of hoping he would.

Instead of staying calm and asking the obvious question—"or else what?"—I burst into tears and fled his office.

I caught sympathetic looks from the office staff on my way out; I was sure they'd overheard the entire thing. They probably got their own share of his outbursts. Once I made it back to my classroom, I closed the door and tried to collect myself. But as soon as I started to calm down, I got angry, furious at myself for crying, furious at him for everything.

By the time I left the building, most of the faculty had already gone home. I got to my car, somehow holding it together just long enough to drive. When I finally walked through the door of my house, I headed straight for the kitchen, poured myself a glass of chardonnay, and said out loud to the empty room: "I'm doing this. I'm going to build and run a bed and breakfast. And Roach can roast in hell."

CHAPTER 13

VIEWPOINTS

It took a couple more issues with Roach to finally push me to leave my career and start a business, but he definitely gave me the initial incentive. I suppose I should be thankful. And I am, until I factor in the Evelyn problem. Maybe I can introduce the two of them. They'd make a perfect couple.

I keep hoping my detective will find something useful, and right on cue, the phone rings. James Bond—aka Jonathan Steele—with some news.

"Sorry it's taken me a while to get back to you. As I mentioned when we met, there were some other cases I had to wrap up first, but I've finally had some time and I have a bit of news."

"Great, what did you find out?"

"I thought maybe I could deliver it in person. I love Yosemite, and I thought maybe we could go on a short hike and I could tell you in some scenic spot."

"Sure. I'd like that. I could definitely use a break from my own head. How about tomorrow?"

Truthfully, I'm looking forward to getting to know him better. I haven't had any kind of date since my divorce. Well, except for that one crazy night I've since filed away in the archives of denial. There were some hints from a couple of the men I worked with, both married. Dropping lines like, "I'm sure you must get lonely sometimes, and if you ever need a shoulder..." (or possibly a penis—that's the real subtext).

When Jonathan arrives, I suggest we hike to Taft Point. It's under two miles one way and I have no idea of his ability to hike or how he handles an altitude of 7,000 feet. The plus side, besides the hike itself, is access to both Washburne and Glacier Point by car after the trek. My concern about his hiking ability is somewhat allayed by the way he dresses: hems and stubborn stains, an old pair of Merrill hiking boots, and a loose long-sleeved shirt, buttoned down the front covering a t-shirt.

"My water and windbreaker are in my daypack, along with some snacks."

So, this isn't his first hike, not even close. I'm especially impressed when he pulls out a beat-up Tilley hat.

"Great. I've packed a picnic, and I'm happy to drive to the trailhead since I know the road so well."

We turn off Wawona Road at Chinquapin and I point out the ranger residence and the trailhead to Badger Pass. After five miles, we pass the entry to the ski area, closed, as usual, waiting for snow that might arrive in December but more realistically in late January... or never.

It's another eight miles to the trailhead, but I pull out on a ridiculously narrow shoulder to show him a spectacular view. I hear him suck in his breath, and who can blame him? It isn't just the view—it's the risk. If he opens his passenger door, he'll drop 1,500 feet straight down.

The back view of Half Dome is obvious, but he doesn't know the peak just below and to the right.

"That's Mount Starr King. Named for Thomas Starr King, a Unitarian minister and political activist in California who supported the Union during the Civil War."

"What range is behind it to the east?" he asks.

"That's the Clark Range and Mt. Clark. Post and Red Peak to the south of it already have a dusting of snow. In front is the Illilouette

Creek drainage area. If the waterfall hasn't totally dried up, I'll show it to you when we get to Washburne Point."

"So, what's the range to the right of the basin?"

"That's Buena Vista Peak in the background and Horse Ridge to the right. Ostrander Lake and the ski hut are below but obscured by the trees. I hike there every summer and ski there in winter."

I can see he's envious as he takes the obligatory photos before we drive further. Gotta love the smartphone with its endless capacity for photos and instant replays. I can't help but think of the old days when my parents would run out of film halfway through a trip—or discover, weeks later, that the perfect shot hadn't turned out at all.

We park at the trailhead, thankfully uncrowded this time of year, and begin the hike to Taft Point. It's still my very favorite place to be in Yosemite, 3,500 feet above the Valley floor. After the fairly level two-mile hike, you leave the narrow trail and pick your way down a slight slope of granite slabs. The terrain is unique, surrounded by crevasses and granite slabs. To the right are crevasses. Every year, at least one visitor, recklessly or tragically, doesn't make it back. Last year, it was a couple on their honeymoon who were taking a selfie at the lip. One step back to get a better view...

Two years ago, I was surprised to see a slack rope between two points, slightly below the rim. A guy was carefully balancing as he moved across the line. He had a safety rope from his body to the line, so in case he fell, it would supposedly catch him and keep him from plunging to his death. It was so scary, I couldn't watch and just turned away, hoping he'd have a safe landing by the time I forced myself to look again.

As Jonathan and I hike, we reach the last crevasse containing two rocks that are trapped forever between the sides, another of the many photo ops. It's a brief climb to the top, where a rail protects you from stepping off the edge. A steel railing mercifully prevents any unintentional plunges. El Capitan is to our left and to our right, Yosemite Falls, now just a trickle.

"I just can't believe this! I've been to Yosemite several times, but I didn't know about this place! I can see why it's your favorite."

I'm impressed that he handles the hike easily and with such enthusiasm.

"We have plenty of time, so would you like to take the six-mile trail that goes along the cliff edge and takes us the back route to Sentinel Dome where we can have lunch?"

"Absolutely! I'll follow you anywhere, Great Leader!"

He's teasing, but it feels nice to be appreciated. The trail crosses Sentinel Creek, now dry at this time of year. In spring, it plunges over the edge and becomes Sentinel Falls.

"I've never heard of it."

"It only flows in the spring. It's pretty narrow, and you have to know exactly where to look. But next time you're here in April or May, look to your left after you pass Yosemite Lodge and you'll see it."

We continue our hike to the base of Sentinel Dome. The climb up over granite slabs doesn't require scrambling. The views are breathtaking—literally and figuratively. From there, besides the full valley view, we can see the Clark Range again and also view the high country of the park, the names of the peaks conveniently given on the circular metal map on top of the dome.

We make it back to the car and take the short drive down, first to Washburne Point where we are above Vernal and Nevada Falls, now barely full, and to our right, Illilouette Falls reduced to a mere trickle. Half Dome is directly in front of us in profile, so totally different from the view from the valley floor.

Jonathan observes, "I like seeing the dome from the side. To me, it looks like a peregrine falcon in his proper place, high above the valley and looking for prey. And, I hear that he does occasionally attack the unwary, throwing a few slabs of rock as a reminder of his domination of this, his world. His beak, the head, his wing a memorial in stone."

As often as I've been there, I've never before seen the resemblance. And now, I'll never forget. I take some time to internalize his description and take an obligatory photo. I make a mental note to ask Lori if she can turn it into a painting—The Washburn Falcon.

I'm not sure what else he might introduce me to as I direct his eyes to the left of Half Dome.

"If you look to the high country north of the valley, you can see the tallest peak, sort of flat on top. That's Mt. Hoffman, the geological center of the park. It's an easy climb from May Lake. It's getting a bit late in the year, though, but if the weather holds, it's a possibility."

"If not, early summer?"

So, I'm not the only one imagining a future. I try to keep the tingles down and simply respond with a nonchalant, "Yeah, that would be nice."

We drive another mile to Glacier Point, where I seldom go. It's true, you're above the valley with only a rail to protect you, but there are always so many people that you don't get any of the solitude you long for to absorb what you're seeing. Jonathan confirms my feelings. "Been here, done that! A bit disappointing after all we've seen."

I like him more with every passing minute.

I drive us back to the house as night comes on. I ask Jonathan if I can fix us something to eat, but he declines.

"I've had a great time today, and I could say I need to get back to work—busy day tomorrow and all that—but that's not the real reason. I think we've both felt a connection. And if I stayed for wine and dinner... well, who knows what we might consider. But you're my client, and I need to keep this professional. Otherwise, neither one of us gets what we need."

He gets in his car and drives away. I stand there watching until his taillights disappear into the trees, an unexpected pang in my chest.

CHAPTER 14

FIRE

We've had three days of rain and thunderstorms, so the return of clear skies feels like a gift. The thunder, amplified by the surrounding mountains, echoes as though we are center stage. Storms are both frightening and exciting. Unlike the coastal forests in northern California, the Sierras are bone-dry in the summer, which always makes me nervous about fires. So when a storm rolls in, we welcome it because it means everything gets a good soaking.

There's still the danger of lightning but at least it is damp. In Yosemite, power lines are buried underground, so while we still have occasional outages, the fire risk from live wires isn't as dire as in other parts of California.

After breakfast, I force myself to tackle my least favorite chore: paperwork, otherwise known as paying bills. At least it's annoying enough to distract me from Evelyn and what she might be brewing next. I notice that my fire insurance has gone up again. Not surprising, but still frustrating. It means I'll have to raise my rates again soon.

In need of a mood reset, I take a glass of iced tea out to the deck. The sunshine has a miraculous way of erasing problems. There is no Evelyn here!

Then, without warning, a bolt of lightning—out of a completely clear, blue sky—strikes a tree in my neighbor's yard. It erupts with burning shards thrown about. I blink, stunned, trying to register what I've just seen. Something on the neighbor's deck catches fire, and I jump into action, grabbing my phone as I run. On the way, I ring the fire gong, an old iron bell many of us have installed at our homes to alert the community of fire. I quickly dial 911 and then the two neighbors I believe to be home as I dash to the fire. The distance seems to have increased—or maybe I'm just running too slowly?

A terrible thought crosses my mind as I run: Do I actually care if their house burns down? They have been pretty obnoxious to me ever since I started this whole project. They rent their place out as a vacation rental, but for some reason, they decided I would destroy the neighborhood by opening a bed and breakfast.

They'd even shown up at my county variance hearing to protest the construction. I hadn't expected them, but there they were, huffing about some such nonsense.

Then, when I applied for a license to serve wine, they protested that too. I could've skipped the paperwork and served a quiet glass or two to guests, and no one would've been the wiser. But I did my research, filed the proper paperwork, and showed up at yet another government board hearing.

Sure enough, there they were again, loudly fretting about "drunks roaming the neighborhood."

I pointed out that I would be home and in control of the serving, while my neighbors had no idea what went on at their place while it was rented out. The commission at least appreciated the irony of the situation.

Between our properties sits a vacant lot, but there is a large variety of weeds and volunteer plants. Legally, we are supposed to clear such vegetation to prevent it from becoming fuel. But we live in a deeply conservative county, where enforcement is lax and people bristle at regulation. So the weeds grow, and so does my irritation.

I think of the danger to my home, even as I run from it to my obnoxious neighbors. A couple of people arrive, and in a short time, we connect a fire hose to the hydrant and the fire is successfully snuffed out. The fire has scorched part of their deck and one room, but the house—

and the rest of the neighborhood—is safe. Without the recent stormy weather, we would have been concerned about the fire spreading below ground level. Pine needles and oak leaves fall to the ground and work their way into the dirt. We call this duff, and it is a fire hazard, as I discovered when raking an area.

Once, while clearing my property, I'd raked a pile of needles and leaves into an open area and set it alight. Armed with a hose, I waited until it burned down, then soaked it thoroughly. Feeling proud of my fire safety skills, I turned to leave—only to spot a thin wisp of smoke coming from the ground several feet away. My small bonfire had lit the duff and had secretly traveled underground. I watered the entire area and waited to be sure the fire was completely out. Lesson learned.

I relax with a cup of tea. Guests are gone. Everything is quiet. But my thoughts drift back to the fire. I have fire insurance on my property, which keeps going up in price every year. I've heard that new home-builders can't even get fire insurance anymore. If there is a devastating fire and my home burns, would I really want to rebuild?

I think of the scarred terrain I pass on the drive to Fresno—nothing living but some low shrubs, even after three years. Gray, bare tree trunks in a barren landscape. Hills once dense with dogwood and pines now totally opened with dead trees mocking the beauty that used to be. Would I want a home in that total bleakness? Would any guests want to be here?

A dark little voice pipes up in the back of my mind: *Well, if "Sis" gets her way, she'll be co-owner of a charred ruin.* Always good to look on the bright side.

Chapter 15

Quaking Aspen

I'm daydreaming about Jonathan while finishing up some paperwork when a brief text from "Dear" Evelyn pops up on my phone:

> Hope you're enjoying the fall color. Thinking of you and how much fun we will have doing business together.

Actually, I *was* enjoying the fall colors—and very deliberately trying not to think about Evelyn. Of course, the moment you try not to think about something, it becomes all you can think about. So, I take a break and step outside to let my eyes soak in the dogwoods and their crimson and orange hues.

Nature does what it always does—calms the noise inside my head.

Back inside, I turn my attention to the upcoming weekend. Lori is coming up Friday night, and then on Saturday, we will head over the Sierras to June Lake to see the quaking aspens in their autumn glory. Most Californians seem to believe that the California border ends at the crest of the Sierra Nevada Mountain range. Not entirely surprising, since the range covers half the length of the state and few highways penetrate to the eastern side. The rise on the west side is gradual, going from valley to low hills to mountains that slowly gain their full height.

But on the east, the Sierras drop off in sheer cliffs to the desert below. The rains that blow in from the ocean rarely make it over the crest, so the eastern side and the state of Nevada beyond are mostly desert— beautiful in their own stark way, but never the lushness of the western slopes. The exception is the narrow band of low hills at the base of the escarpment where quaking aspen thrive in abundance.

They remind me of birch trees on steroids. The trunks are white, like birch, with horizontal dark lines and patches that give them a particular beauty, but they are thicker. The leaves are similar to birch but broad and heart-shaped, fluttering in even the faintest breeze. Around mid-October, they explode into vibrant shades of yellow, gold, orange, and burgundy—a photographer's paradise. Lori has never seen them in peak color, and I can't wait to share their beauty with her—and see what she might later turn into a painting.

When she arrives, she is full of questions about my cryptic recent messages. Over a glass or two of wine, I spill the story—Evelyn's threat, my new detective, and everything in between. She is almost in shock with disbelief, until I mention that I've hired someone to investigate Evelyn.

"Did you sleep with him?" she asks, deadpan.

"What?! I hired a guy to investigate Evelyn, not to sleep with him!"

"So, like I said, did you have sex? I'm worried about you. You haven't been with a man since you and Jack split three years ago. Your most important asset is drying up."

I don't respond. I'd never told her—or anyone—about that one regrettable one-off last year that I am still trying to forget.

But I'm not really surprised at her question, as a great deal of Lori's life revolves around sex. Though she goes by Lori, her full name was Lorelei Lee, named after a character in the 1925 novel, *Gentlemen Prefer Blondes,* by Anita Loos.

In German folklore, Lorelei was a siren with flowing blonde hair who lured sailors to their deaths on the Rhine. My Lori doesn't kill her men—she just sleeps with them. Lots of them.

I should amend that. I doubt they got any sleep at all. I've never quite understood how she does it. She's attractive, but certainly not beautiful. She does have large breasts—my mother once said she was "certainly well-endowed"—and men seem to orbit her. Though she's 42, her age range for romantic partners is anywhere between twenty and seventy, or as she puts it, "I like variety." She is unapologetically direct.

"Face it! I like to fuck."

We once went to a conference together and were on a twenty-minute flight from Los Angeles to John Wayne Airport in Orange County. We were the last to board and weren't seated together. When we deplaned, she introduced me to her seatmate.

"This is John," she said, giving his arm a little squeeze. (I call all of Lori's men John—there are too many to keep track.)

"He's getting his car and taking us to the hotel," she said brightly.

As he dutifully trotted off to get his Cadillac (Lori's Johns often had money), she said, "Do you need to go to our room right away? Maybe grab a drink in the bar first? Just give me a little time..."

"Holy shit, Lori! That was a twenty-minute flight. What did you do? Grab his crotch?"

She shrugged. "Well... it saves a lot of time."

That's Lori for you. Now we are road-tripping again—just the two of us this time, no Johns in tow.

The drive east is stunning. We take the Wawona Road into Yosemite Valley and spend a bit of time enjoying the views. Leaving the valley, we climb to Highway 120, which takes us over the mountains. Yosemite Creek, the source of the famous falls, flows through a forested valley. The road winds past Yosemite Creek, dropping into narrow valleys, and rising again with expansive views of the higher peaks.

We pass the trailhead to Lukens Lake. I make a mental note that this would be a perfect hike for Jonathan. You almost always see a bear, and in spring and summer, the walk around the lake is a wildflower paradise.

I refocus on driving and explain more of the terrain to Lori. At Olmstead Point, we stop to admire the view of Half Dome and Tenaya Lake, with Tenaya Peak looming above.

"You can see Cathedral Peak behind the lake."

It's a favorite climb, though I've never had the nerve to do it. Maybe next summer we can do the loop around it.

In Tuolumne Meadows, you start on the trail to the Cathedral Lakes, then veer off and follow a creek up to Budd Lake. Here you're at the east base of Cathedral Peak, the south base of Unicorn, and north of Echo Peaks.

"We'll hike over a low ridge, descending to upper Cathedral Lake, and return by the trail," I tell Lori. "If there's time, we can go to the other lakes and even descend on a trail that takes us down to the highway, but a few miles from our car. I'll show you as we drive by."

"So, how do we get back to the car?"

"Hitchhike."

"Hitchhike! You're kidding! Isn't it dangerous? People think I live dangerously since I tend to go to bed with relative strangers, but I don't hitchhike."

"Possibly. But there aren't any side roads, and some curves force the driver to slow down, so you can always jump out."

"Whoopie!"

"Seriously. It's sort of the way things are done here. If I see someone hitching, I stop and pick them up. Never have a problem, though there is the one time I picked up the 'Squirrel Lady.'"

"This I've got to hear!"

"I'll tell you when we stop for lunch in Lee Vining. Too many sights to point out in this area."

After passing Tenaya Lake, we climb a bit and then descend to Tuolumne Meadows: a treasure at any time of year. The broad meadows and forests of lodgepole pine are bisected by the Tuolumne River. Cathedral and Unicorn Peaks post guard to the south, Lembert Dome rises in the center, and Mt. Gibbs and Dana, 13,000 feet-plus, mark the height of the range to the east.

I point out Pothole Dome on our left and suggest we do the short hike to the top, as the views are even more breathtaking. I point out the winding river and share a memory.

"I skied here last year with a group from the cross-country Winter Club. We spent two nights here in a cabin, and on the layover day, some of us skied over here to Pothole Dome and climbed it. Fabulous views and an easy ski down. The more adventurous, or maybe just more experienced, skied partly up Unicorn. A bit too frightening for me to attempt."

Back in the car, we are soon at the Cathedral Lakes trailhead. We continue to where the highway crosses the river.

"Let's stop for a snack and put our feet in the water," Lori suggests.

"Good idea. Let's take the short walk to Soda Springs."

The water there is fizzy, hence the name. We don't drink the fizzy water—Park Service signs warn it might be contaminated—but we splash around and eat our snacks beside the river. I'm not sure if the sign is accurate or a reflection of an over-solicitous governing agency, but we behave ourselves and stick to our own water bottles.

We drive another nine miles to Tioga Pass, the eastern entrance to the park. We are at the base of Mount Dana, which, at 13,061 feet, is the second-highest peak in the park. (Mt. Lyell bests Dana by a mere 53 feet.) Then we descend rapidly to the desert below and the small town of Lee Vining. There, we stop at the gas station and the Whoa Nellie Diner for the obligatory fish tacos.

And, as promised, I tell Lori the tale of the Squirrel Lady.

CHAPTER 16

THE SQUIRREL LADY

I was heading home from Yosemite Valley last spring when I spotted a woman hitchhiking. We just had a cold snap and she looked like she had participated. She looked like she'd been living in it—shivering, with a heavy duffel slung over her shoulder. I pulled over, and she climbed in. We drove for a while without speaking, which started to feel awkward, so I decided to strike up a conversation.

"So, why are you in Yosemite? Are you camping?"

"Sort of. It's just too cold, so I thought I'd come back in a week or so."

"Are you by yourself? That could get a bit lonely. What do you do with all that free time? Do you climb?"

"Oh, no. I don't want to climb. Too dangerous. I just sort of sit around and enjoy the views. I do have a hobby; I carve. I make little animal figures, usually bears, to sell to tourists."

"Interesting. What kind of wood do you like to work with?"

"I like fruit woods best. I can't use myrtle wood at all, despite how pretty it is."

"I have a myrtle wood bowl, so I know what you mean. The wood is gorgeous."

"You better watch it. Keep it locked up at night or it can run away."

At that point, I started to wonder if maybe I shouldn't have picked her up. That's when it hit me—this had to be the infamous Squirrel Lady. The rangers had mentioned her before. She was known for wandering the park, often begging for a space in tourists' tents or asking for meals when she didn't have any money. Her carvings were apparently quite good, but she didn't have a license to sell them inside the park, so she was nearly always violating some rule. Still, she didn't seem dangerous—just... off. Confused about how things worked. I'd studied music therapy in college and worked with people navigating mental illness, so I was more intrigued than afraid.

She turned to me and said, "Most people think I'm crazy. And maybe they're right. I wasn't always like this. I started college at UC Berkeley and rented a room in an old Victorian house. The ancient owner had recently died in that room, so it was cheap. I didn't believe in ghosts, so I wasn't worried. But I should've been. The dead woman started creeping into my brain and body. Sometimes, I just become her. It's nothing I can control. I've just learned to accept her presence. She liked to quilt, so I've taken that up—along with carving."

She was speaking so clearly, so calmly, I felt myself drawn in. I asked where she intended to go, and she said, "Oakhurst."

It was out of my way, but I drove her there anyway. When we arrived, she said, "You've been so kind, I want to give you my quilt patterns."

She handed me about twenty nine-inch fabric squares, each with a simple design drawn in black marker.

"I can't take your lovely squares!"

"Please. When I work with them, she invades my body!"

I sorted through them. "Look—some of these are round, and others are pointy. I'll take the round ones. I think maybe those are the ones where you get trapped—circling around with no way out. But you should keep the pointed ones. They're spears and knives. You can use them to fend her off."

"You really get it," she said softly, and climbed out of the car.

I never saw her again. But later, at a party, I told the story to the magistrate judge and suggested that if she ever ended up in court again, maybe they should appoint someone to help her. Her brain wasn't wired for the logic of the legal system.

Lori and I head south and take the June Lake loop, winding through grove after grove of glowing aspen. Their leaves shimmer in a thousand variations of gold, rust, orange, and burgundy.

We stop often so Lori can take photos or make quick sketches. Eventually, we find a cozy place to stay for the night. I promise her the colors will be even more spectacular in the morning light. Over a couple glasses of wine, the conversation turns personal, as it always does with Lori.

"I'm hoping this trip will set me on a new career path. Since you left, Roach has decided to focus on me. It's constant badgering, questioning everything I do, none of which is done to his satisfaction. He can't get it that art isn't a competitive sport. To him, if it's not a competition with a ribbon at the end, it's a waste of time."

She mimics his voice: "Why can't you just teach poster design so the kids can enter competitions? Why are you wasting time with useless things like painting and printmaking? That's not a job—it's a hobby for rich people. Anybody can throw a pot. I say throw them all out and focus on winning! Winning will bring glory to Winston High."

She lets out a long, exasperated sigh. "I mean, really?"

I assumed it was just me, and that once I left, he would settle down and do his job. Obviously, he can't get his head around anything beyond competitive sports, and it is impossible to educate him at this stage. If it isn't competitive, measurable, or connected to his own glory, it doesn't matter. It is maddening.

Lori is a really fine painter and she'll probably do okay making her way as a professional artist. I worry about my other former colleagues. Is Roach going after the band teacher now? Crafts? Is science even safe?

Few things are more frustrating than watching something so completely wrong happen and feeling helpless to stop it.

I remind her, again, that she is a fabulous artist and that she will have success in her new career.

She gives me a sheepish smile and says, "It's just really scary. Starting over when you're over forty... which reminds me, you've never told me the full story of what you did once you thought about leaving."

CHAPTER 17

ARCHITECT

Another run-in with Roach was pushing me to make decisions.

When I got back from Christmas vacation, he was on a roll again. The previous principal had asked me to head up a discipline committee, hoping we could figure out how to get some of the more difficult students engaged with the school, rather than constantly being in trouble.

My committee zeroed in on the "Non-Privilege List"—a district-mandated list of students who had received two or more "unsatisfactories" on their report cards and, as a result, were barred from participating in any school activities. The problem was that these were the kids who never participated in anything to begin with—not class, not sports, nada.

So, we flipped the strategy and told the kids that if they signed up to work with any adult at the school, a teacher, a custodian, a secretary, or someone in the cafeteria, and worked two hours a week for four weeks, they could earn their way off the list. The idea was that if they felt more connected to the school, more like they belonged, they'd behave like they had a stake in it.

It worked. The kids got involved, the list got shorter, and there were fewer repeats. Of course, Roach couldn't let someone else's success stand.

"I'm replacing the current discipline policy, which is far too lenient, with a zero-tolerance plan."

Zero tolerance meant that breaking the rules, any rule, automatically triggered a punishment. We were given a list of "crimes" and "punishments" and were instructed to post them prominently in our classrooms. We were to read the list aloud to our students every week during first period.

Several teachers, including me, pointed out the obvious: We were working with kids, not adult criminals. We already had an effective discipline system, but none of that mattered.

"You're wrong," Roach said flatly. "If pupils don't learn the rules and obey them, they will most certainly grow up to be criminals."

No supporting data. No nuance. Just a rigid mindset that believed school should be a boot camp. Apparently, we were supposed to help these kids by making school so miserable they'd eventually drop out, thus ensuring the exact outcome we were supposedly trying to prevent.

That was when I knew I had to seriously rethink my future in education. I started making a plan—not because I was ready to walk away immediately, but because I needed a vision for something else, something better.

Turning the house into a bed and breakfast seemed like the answer. It would allow me to live in a version of my beloved part-time home and hopefully earn enough to support myself.

Lori came up the following weekend and helped sketch some initial floor plan ideas. I took her drawings and my stack of photographs to three different architects, hoping to get a sense of what might be possible.

Two of them didn't even hesitate. "Tear it down," they said. "Start fresh." Technically, that was illegal. County code required that at least one wall remain standing to qualify as a remodel rather than a rebuild.

However, I was assured that the county board always granted a variance. There would be a fee, of course, not only to the county but also to the architect for presenting my case with all the necessary documentation.

Neither one seemed to consider my emotional attachment to this house, and how bulldozing it would destroy memories of so many wonderful family times.

The third architect, Donna, was different. "Your house has good bones," she said, running her hand along one of the photos, "and good memories. Let's start by thinking about what's going to draw guests here—and what's going to make them want to come back."

We both agreed that the view and the word Yosemite were the primary attractions. "So, I think we need to place the guest rooms in the back overlooking the creek," she continued. "And I suggest keeping the guest accommodations on the ground floor, since it's annoying to everyone to have suitcases bumping up and down the stairs at all hours. The view from upstairs will be better, of course. The upstairs can be for dining, maybe near a big window. We can add a terrace where people can enjoy breakfast, and that terrace floor will double as a roof for the guest patio, making it usable even during bad weather."

"But what about the front of the house? Those tiny windows have to go. How do we bring in more light?"

"I'll play with the options," she said. "I think a glass front door will help. And if we place the stairs in the center, we can allow light to filter down from the living and dining areas. We may even add a skylight."

At our next meeting, she brought tentative floor plans for both levels. I studied them, but I could feel the hesitation in my own voice when I said, "I think this could work."

"I know it's hard to visualize space from a two-dimensional floor plan," she said kindly. "So, I'm going to build a scale model out of foam core. That way, you can really see it."

She built the floors as separate pieces that could be stacked, giving a good sense of how the light world works. It was amazing.

When I was a little girl, Dad built me a two-story dollhouse that had a missing back wall, so you could peek into all the rooms. Donna's version had a removable roof so you could peer down into the rooms. She even added tiny paper cutouts of two-dimensional furnishings.

Though unlike my dollhouse, where the furniture seemed real, these were paper cutouts that just sat on the floor. But you could see just how much space a bed or chair would take up in the room.

I was delighted with my new toy, not only because it brought back happy memories, but because I now believed this could really happen. It was more than just a visual aid—it was proof. I ran my fingers along the little model's terrace and smiled.

I was ready for the next step: hiring a contractor.

CHAPTER 18

FINDING A CONTRACTOR

I picked four contractors at random, just searching the local areas online. The interviews were fascinating and surprisingly instructive. I was entering a culture I'd never experienced before.

My parents hadn't worked with their hands, outside of gardening. Neither had my husband, nor I.

When something went wrong with the plumbing, you called a plumber. If the electricity failed, you called an electrician. It would never have occurred to any of us to figure out what was wrong, let alone fix it ourselves.

Electricity felt like some kind of invisible magic—powerful and mysterious. We could change a lightbulb, sure, but that was about it.

I'll admit I had expected to be interviewing men with limited education but a lot of practical experience—an old stereotype I quickly had to discard. Of the four I interviewed, only one hadn't gone to university, and he'd gone to a community college instead.

Of the other two, Jack had completed university, majoring in Philosophy, and the other, Phil, had nearly completed a degree in Architecture before dropping out during his final semester.

The other contractor was a woman—educated, competent, and a

very welcome surprise. She was feminine in both appearance and manner, and I immediately felt like I'd be comfortable working with her.

I submitted the plans to all four, asking for bids. Secretly, I was hoping the woman would come in lowest, but Jack submitted the lowest estimate, by quite a bit, which put me in a bit of a quandary.

I know it sounds silly, but my ex-husband's name was Jack, and the name alone stirred up unpleasant emotions. Did I really need another *jack*ass in my life?

It probably helped that he was good-looking, but not at all like my former husband. He was good-looking, but not in a polished or intimidating way. Medium height—maybe 5'10"—with the kind of fitness that comes from hard physical work. Deep brown eyes and lighter brown hair, streaked blond from working outdoors.

I guessed his age at around 40, a few years younger than me. I decided that despite his name, I could work with him. So, we sat down together going over all the details of the bid.

"I think it'll take about nine months to a year to get the permits and finish the place. We'll need a small variance, but once we get county board approval, we can move forward with the building permit and start construction."

It sounded simple enough—until the hearing. I walked into a room full of locals, most of whom I'd never met. At first, I assumed they were there for another item on the agenda. But no—I was the headliner.

Several people stood to comment on the variance, which was so minor, it really shouldn't have required a board hearing at all. The variance gave the locals a chance to vent on several issues that had little to do with me, and I became their random, unfortunate target.

I understand that people get uncomfortable with change. But after everything I'd just gone through with Roach, I wasn't ready for yet another public flogging. Thankfully, Jack was beside me and remained calm and composed, answering the complaints with reason and clarity. I was furious—boiling over—and would have been incapable of dealing with the stupidity had I been on my own.

"If she adds a second story, it will ruin my view," one woman complained. She was my neighbor from across the street.

Jack calmly answered, "Ma'am, you have a two-story house. My client has the same right."

"Her real plans are to buy up other properties and open a hotel."

Right, on a schoolteacher's salary.

"We already have enough tourists invading our area," grumbled a man who, ironically, owned five vacation rentals.

"Does she plan to serve booze in her B&B like so many do? That will mean drunks loose on our streets."

I hadn't expected any of this and was quickly approaching my boiling point. Jack kept fielding the absurdity like a pro.

"She may decide to offer a glass of wine in the evening, not liquor," he replied, "but she'll be on-site with her guests. Unlike many of you who run short-term or vacation rentals and don't monitor your guests at all, she'll actually be monitoring the activity on her property. I've heard complaints about loud, drunken parties—and none of them were coming from her place."

It went on and on until even Jack started to lose his cool. Faced with all that local anger, the board denied the variance. Jack and I both badly needed a beer, but there was no way I would go into any local bar in the county seat.

So, we drove half an hour to the next town and found a quiet spot for a couple of frosty pale ales. Over drinks, I vented all my frustrations.

I realized that I had become completely committed to opening a bed and breakfast—and now it felt like my neighbors might keep me from doing it.

Jack, who was ever calm, just nodded. "I think we should just let things settle down for a month. The neighbors are probably a bit embarrassed about their rudeness to you today, and they'll want to put it behind them."

"You seem awfully chipper for a guy who just had his job shot down."

"All part of the game. I think I told you I was a philosophy major in college and that I worked in Europe for three years." He laughed. "It's all part of the game. I think I told you I was a philosophy major. I even spent a few years working in Europe."

"You did. And I'm still surprised you ended up in construction."

"Here's the deal for me. In philosophy, you rummage around and come up with lots of possible answers but seldom see any application. In contracting, you actually build something. Your ideas are realized in a concrete form. So now, I often work on projects that have conflicting ideas that need to be solved, but when that happens, I have something actual to look at. I think it is the best fusion of both worlds. It makes more sense than you'd think," he said.

"Okay," I said. "So what's your strategy now?"

"Simple. We tweak the design so we don't need a variance and resubmit to the building department. In the meantime, you should head up to your place every weekend. Let the neighbors get to know you. Show them you want to be part of the community. Eventually, all this will blow over. There's probably some kind of community group that helps shape local decisions—join it."

And he was right, of course.

We started construction that July. The goal was to have the house "closed in" before the snow fell—usually November or December. Most of the interior work could continue over the winter, but things like the exterior finish would have to wait until spring. Jack figured we'd wrap up by late April or May, giving me just enough time to furnish the place and open for guests in July.

It was the perfect setup. I could run the B&B every summer, maybe during holidays too. It would bring in extra income and keep me in the mountains—the place I loved—during the best part of the year.

Telling Lori about the beginnings of my new career is unexpectedly relaxing.

The wine helps, too.

We get up early the next morning so she can capture more photos. We drive back through Lee Vining and then head north to the Lundy Canyon turnoff. We park and begin walking through grove after grove of aspen, their colors even more vivid than the ones we'd seen near June Lake—if that's possible.

Toward the end of the canyon, we rise above the trees and stand awestruck. Below us flows a river of gold, orange, and crimson. I point out the trail that comes down the escarpment from Saddlebag Lake, which lies just outside the park at an elevation of over 9,000 feet. A waterfall still flows this late in the year—a testament to the deep winter snowpack.

What a great weekend. Lori is starting to see a path forward, and I was able to erase Evelyn.

Almost.

CHAPTER 19

RETURNING HOME

On the drive back, I suggest we stop and take the one-mile hike to Lukens Lake, which gives us a good break. Lori is enthusiastic, hoping we might spot a bear or two.

We don't have to wait long. As we pull into the parking area, we see a large cinnamon-colored adult bear ambling nearby. It vanishes quickly into the trees, but it still counts.

The hike to the lake is pleasantly downhill, and we circle the shoreline before returning on the same path.

"Lori, I promise to bring you back in early summer when the damselflies start to emerge," I say as we walk. "They rise from their pupae stage on the reeds—these delicate, blue creatures, hundreds, maybe thousands, all lifting off together. At first, they look like lifeless brown casings stuck to the stalks, and then, suddenly, a shimmering cerulean cloud takes flight. You'd love it. It's absolutely magical."

The rest of the trip back is filled with easy conversation and reminiscing—memories, old colleagues, former students. By the time we turn off the main road and into Yosemite West, Evelyn has finally vacated my brain.

But that peace, of course, doesn't last. Evelyn is standing in front of my house. She doesn't even wait for me to get out of the car before launching in.

"Where have you been? I thought we were running a business here, but it's hard to make money if you don't rent out the rooms."

Before I can respond, Lori steps in, voice smooth as silk. "I don't believe we've met," she says, charm oozing from every syllable.

"I'm Evelyn, the sister! Surely you've heard about me! Monica and I have the same daddy!"

"Really?" Lori replies. "Not a lot of family resemblance, but you never know. I had no idea you were a part owner—your name doesn't appear on any of the paperwork."

"What paperwork?" Evelyn's face twitches.

Turning to me, still the vision of utter control, "Haven't you told your sister about the Costa Rica property? I bet she'd love it there!"

"Costa Rica?!" Evelyn's voice cracks on the words. The shock on her face is pure gold. I have to bite my lip to keep from laughing.

"I'm sure your sister has told you, or maybe"—turning to me—"you were saving it as a surprise? Family secrets are so much fun. But this is such a bad time—I'm running late, and there's a stack of paperwork to finish. I'm sure your sister will get back to you with all the details. You're going to love Costa Rica!"

Without missing a beat, she ushers me into the house, and we barely make it past the front door before dissolving into uncontrollable laughter, practically peeing our pants laughing so hard.

"Lori! You are great! How did you come up with that line so fast?"

"I've been dabbling in improv lately—strictly amateur stuff, but it's a blast. They present you with a scenario, and you have to come up with an immediate response. Becoming your real estate agent? Piece of cake. The Costa Rica line just popped out. Hopefully, it throws her off long enough for her to either back off or get so aggressive she does something stupid enough to make legal action easier."

Still giggling, she adds, "We should walk the neighborhood. Make sure she isn't lurking in anyone's driveway. If I get home late, it's no biggie. Actually, maybe I'll ditch school tomorrow and stay the night. You could use a little backup."

I help her solidify the decision by promising to make Hangtown Fry for dinner—an old '49er breakfast that works just as well for dinner, assuming you like oysters.

That evening, we eat, we drink, and we talk—reminiscing about the chaos and comedy of building the bed and breakfast and marveling at just how far I have come.

Chapter 20

Construction

The building permit came by mid-July, and if everything went smoothly, the house would be finished by the following May.

My plan was to keep teaching for a few more years, renting the place out during the summer.

I figured I'd need both my teaching salary and whatever income the B&B brought in to start paying off the construction loan. After a few good seasons with the business established, I could take early retirement, work eight months of the year, and maybe spend part of the winter on the coast.

Or maybe Costa Rica?

Well, part of the plan actually worked.

I assumed that somehow things would just happen, and I would eventually move into my cozy new home, and then open my business, sort of like how most people buy a house. You know the drill: drive through new neighborhoods, tour model homes, choose a layout, pick flooring and appliances before the move, and then—voilà—everything's finished, the moving company shows up, furniture goes exactly where you want it, and... "Honey! We're home!"

Yeah. Not quite that easy.

First, you actually need money to build. I'd blithely assumed that when I walked into the bank in March, the manager would see my charming vision of a bed and breakfast and all the potential income and happily hand over the construction loan.

"Hey, Mr. Banker, can I borrow about $350,000 to build my dream house? It's going to be a thriving business. I'll totally be able to pay you back once the guests arrive!"

To their credit, none of the bankers laughed in my face. But after being turned down by the third bank, I realized I'd have to find another way.

Selling my house in Winston was the most obvious solution—but that would leave me without a place to live. Then it hit me—the answer had been under my nose all along.

I called Tommy.

We'd both done reasonably well with the inheritance after our parents died, though mine was less because I'd received the house, which had been appraised lower than its true emotional value. I'd planned to use my cushion for furnishing the B&B and covering the inevitable costs that would pop up.

"Tommy, I hate to ask, but I'm having trouble getting financing. I could sell my home in Winston, but I need somewhere to live during the school year."

"What took you so long to call? My inheritance is just sitting in the bank. Gioia and I do well out here in D.C. I'll lend you what you need, and you can start repaying once the business is up and running."

And that was that. It was that simple. Time to get moving on this project.

Jack and I met for a long meeting about next steps and how everything would come together.

"First, obviously, is to take down most of your old house, leaving all four walls if we can."

I gasped. The reality of dismantling that house hit hard. So many memories tied to those walls.

"Next is the foundation. Your place, like all of Yosemite, sits on granite. We've got decomposed granite and years of plant buildup on top, but underneath, it's rock solid. We'll dig down where needed, drill into the granite, and pour cement. Then we either reinforce walls or frame the place. Then it's a race to get the siding and roof on before the snow flies."

Jack continued, "Once the place is closed in, we can get the plumbing, the heating, and the electric in. Once the wallboard goes up—you'll start to see real rooms. That's the best part—when you can see the space and start imagining the furniture, the guests, the life inside it."

Most weekends, I drove up to Yosemite to check on progress. We left all four walls standing—barely. They would be structurally reinforced and reworked to allow for new windows and the second story.

The front entry was a challenge. That flat, uninviting facade had to go. The architect and I played with pediments and balconies, but it still wasn't right. Jack suggested we recess the front door, slanting the side wall to give a natural sense of welcome. Glass in the side walls and front door would allow more light into the front of the house, making it more inviting to guests. It was perfect.

The building department approved the change without issue. As the framing went up, the house began taking shape. It was hard to visualize the finished space through the skeletal frame—you could see right through all the walls—but it was happening.

When the electrical and plumbing lines were in place, I took photos of all the walls and carefully labeled them in case repairs were needed after the sheet rock was in place. That was Jack's idea—the contractor, not my ex-husband, whom I now refer to as my *was*band, or—more accurately—jackass.

Sorry, but two Jacks in my life is too many.

I enjoyed working with Jack. He had an easy manner, and when there were glitches or major mistakes by workers, he corrected them without losing his cool.

One Friday evening, I arrived with a six-pack in an ice chest and a batch of CHILI CHEESE BALLS. We sat on a stack of lumber, beers in hand, and assessed how things were going. Despite the usual issues—late materials, endless unexpected costs—I was having the time of my life. I began to see why a person might choose construction over philosophy.

When the sheetrock went up on the walls, I could feel I was really building a home for me and a business for my guests. Access to the second floor was via ladder at that point. The workers hated seeing me climb it, but I didn't mind.

The higher ceilings gave the rooms a spacious feel and let in even more light.

There were lots of decisions that I had to make, and I felt wildly unprepared, like how to decide on paint colors or if the walls should be covered in another material, such as wood paneling or wallpaper. Roofing material and color. Siding? Window trim?

We were both pleased about how everything was going smoothly, and the conversation wandered over to more personal talk.

"I'm curious," I asked one evening. "Why would a college grad with a degree in philosophy become a contractor?"

"I actually got a master's degree and a teaching position in a junior college. It was a good job, but I wasn't satisfied. Couldn't quite put my finger on why. I spent most of my spare time on building projects, ranging from model airplanes to working at construction sites. After a few years, and a couple relationships that didn't go anywhere, I took off for Europe." He didn't say much more about the relationships, and I didn't pry. It wasn't my business. I spent three years there in a variety of countries. Turns out philosophers are actually employable—especially in Europe. They hire us to assess the social consequences of big projects before they start. Who knew? Definitely not me. In America, we just plow ahead and deal with the fallout later."

That made me laugh. "I had no idea either."

"Am I talking too much?" he asked.

"Not at all! I find it really interesting."

I was being mostly truthful. Okay, partly truthful.

Jack was interesting. Not tall, dark, or handsome like my wasband, but he was nice to be around and talk to. I felt a bit of stirring in my body that said, *Maybe... maybe this could go somewhere.*

"So, I came back to America and got another teaching job and realized at the end of the semester what was wrong, what I couldn't quite identify before. Philosophy, particularly in the classroom, is never really concrete, and I like the reality of a finished product. I like figuring out how things get put together. I wanted a way to work with my brain and my hands. So, I came to California because of the climate and worked for a variety of contractors while I studied for the state exam. I settled near Yosemite because I liked to climb in the summer and ski in the winter. I've been contracting for three years, and now you have my whole history, and I think it's time I shut up, finish my beer, and head home."

He stood, drank the last of his beer, and walked to his truck.

I realized I'd completely forgotten to ask if he was married.

Then again... maybe that was for the best.

CHAPTER 21

A Different Kind of
Classroom

Part of reminiscing with Lori was remembering what it felt like to return to teaching that September. I'd been hoping—really hoping—that I could adjust to Roach, but I wasn't confident I could handle it. Maybe, I thought, if the Powers That Be were merciful, they'd transfer him. Or better yet, promote him. If *The Peter Principle* had any truth to it, he was due for a move upward—where, as the book suggested, "cream rises to the top, then sours." Superintendent Roach had a terrifying ring to it, but at least he'd be out of *my* building.

That year, I had a new teaching schedule, and I wasn't thrilled. Roach had slashed one of my choral classes and assigned me to a study hall instead. I've always thought "study hall" was one of the dumbest ideas in education. Kids can study at home. School should be a place where they actually learn something. And don't even get me started on the name—it's a complete misnomer. There's never any studying going on in study hall.

Of course, other teachers argued that there had to be somewhere to send the difficult kids. My usual response was, "Teach so well they want to stay in your class." That typically earned an eye roll or a sarcastic retort like, "That's easy for you to say—you teach music. Kids like music. I teach math (or English or history), and it's a different story."

And okay, they weren't wrong. There *are* times, no matter how great your lesson is, that a subject just doesn't feel interesting to a kid. So, some of them entertain themselves and their peers by creating chaos.

Now, with Roach's new zero tolerance discipline policy, I could see why study halls were necessary. At the rate we were booting kids out of class, we'd need one—or several—every period.

The one perk of being assigned to study hall was that, at least for the first week, there were no students. But they started trickling in soon enough, getting kicked out one class at a time.

Most of them were boys, though a few thoroughly unpleasant girls joined, too. Honestly, I preferred the boys. Beneath the bravado and contempt, most had an internal compass that nudged them toward being slightly nicer to female teachers. A pattern emerged: The boys who ended up with me were almost always kicked out by male teachers. I figured it was a version of the old cub-versus-lion-king dynamic.

By the end of week three, I had ten "inmates"—eight boys, two girls. When the headcount hit fifteen the next week, it struck me: I was no longer a teacher. I was a prison guard. And I hated it.

So, I tried bribery.

The study hall was housed in one of the music rooms—larger spaces with great acoustics and several little practice rooms off to the side. That kind of design is perfect for students singing or playing instruments. Not so great when the soundtrack is foul language and yelling.

Up until this point in my career, I'd never really had discipline problems. Now, suddenly, I had a room full of them and no idea what to do. In my regular classes, the kids *wanted* to be there. And those who didn't were usually kept in check by their classmates. Music is self-policing that way. I hadn't realized how lucky I'd been.

I dreaded going to study hall more than the kids dreaded being there. For them, it was a break from math or English. For me, it was torture. Desperate to maintain some semblance of sanity—and avoid shouting at teenagers—I turned to food.

I promised that anyone who behaved all week would get treats on Friday. I brought my famous brownies, fully expecting to win hearts and minds with chocolate.

What I got instead were complaints.

"I'm gluten intolerant."

"I'm allergic to chocolate."

"My mom says I can't have sugar."

"He swiped my brownie!"

Clearly, a new strategy was needed.

I decided to fall back on what I knew best. I was, after all, a music teacher.

So, I would teach music.

CHAPTER 22

MUSIC HALL

"How many of you can play the guitar or piano?"

Three boys and a girl raised their hands, so I got four guitars out of the storage area and asked them to show me what they could do. They were all surprisingly good. I say "surprisingly" because these kids were supposed to be the dregs—the ones who couldn't do anything right.

The rest of the class settled down and listened quietly for at least five minutes, but then they grew restless. And we all know from the movies that when the natives get restless, danger lies just ahead.

To head that off, I asked my new musicians if they knew anything about the Blues. They didn't. So, I explained that the Blues always told stories—stories of being oppressed, down and out, or steeped in some other kind of sadness. I played a Blues riff on the piano and then sang *St. Louis Blues*. Not a sound from my "audience" at first... and then they clapped.

Most of them had no idea I could sing—or anything else about me, really. They didn't know I was a music teacher. To them, I was just the bitch in front of the room, and their job was to make my life miserable.

To keep the momentum going, I suggested they try their hand at writing a Blues song. We talked about what the song could be about, which prompted lots of responses about the things that were wrong in their lives. I divided them into small groups, each led by one of the guitar players. I showed the guitarists a simple chord progression common to the Blues and sent the groups to the practice rooms to start writing.

Five minutes before the bell, I called them back to check on their progress. They were amazing. Every group had a strong start to a song. I suggested they continue working on it the next day and be ready to perform the day after that. Instead of the usual disdain, I saw excitement in their eyes.

And I was thoroughly enjoying myself.

Then I got called in to report to Roach at the end of the day. I had no idea what he could possibly want, but I knew it couldn't be good. And I was right.

He had been evaluating all my choral performances from the past spring, and in his eyes, the results were disappointing. Which meant they were going to be disappointing for me, too. I hadn't finished first. I hadn't won. And how do you explain to someone supposedly educated —and completely clueless—that music is not a competitive sport?

He pointed out that my colleague Stan, the band director, had won the spring marching band competition. I tried to explain that, while it was called a competition, it wasn't truly a contest. Stan had earned a first place, but it wasn't like a football game with a single winner and a loser. In fact, there could be multiple firsts—two or even three.

But I might as well have been talking to a wall.

He pointed out, correctly, that I had not received a first place, and he expected that to change. I was to come in first. I was to *win* for Winston. Otherwise, he would ask to have me transferred.

Well, crap.

At least study hall was going well. The kids had dubbed themselves "The Zeros." When a new Zero arrived, I integrated them into one of my six groups. The groups were based on the fact that we had only six practice rooms, and each could only hold six or seven people. We were reaching capacity.

I asked the kids if they had been spreading the word about our music study hall, and from the averted eyes and sudden fascination with their laps, I had my answer.

"Okay," I said. "For those of you kicked out of math, you're going to have a math problem today. What is 6 x 7?"

"36."

"50."

"45."

And finally, a wee voice: "42?"

I asked again if they'd been telling friends what we were doing in study hall. Several assured me they had. I explained that if too many students showed up, I'd have no choice but to run a traditional study hall and stop the music activities. There was only so much space—and only so many guitars.

They groaned.

"Let's keep this very secretive," I said, "or it may have to end. And I don't think any of us want that."

Even the couple of stoners, who often couldn't focus long enough to finish a single lyric, were alert enough to agree.

By the end of the semester, I was confident I had turned some kids around. I believed they'd be able to stay in regular classes without being disruptive.

CHAPTER 23

ROACH AGAIN

The second semester started, and once again, I was assigned a study hall. I was surprised to see some returnees from the previous semester—I thought I'd helped launch them onto a path of good citizenship. I had questions.

"Manuel, Fred, Jorge! Why are you back here so soon? I thought we agreed you'd learned how to behave properly in your regular classes."

Their words tumbled over one another, but the gist was clear. "We were learning so much more here."

Jorge added, "I don't see how I'll ever use algebra—even if I could actually do it."

Fred summed it up best: "When you're an adult talking to people, do they ever ask you to define a noun or diagram a sentence?"

A few had figured out how to behave just badly enough to get removed from class, but not so badly as to be suspended or expelled. I was learning that these kids, whom many staff members considered too dumb to tie their shoes, were actually quite sophisticated when it came to understanding school and working the system.

I knew I was onto something important about how kids process information, but I wasn't sharp enough to figure out how to put it to wider use with other teachers. So, I decided to stick with what seemed to work.

"Okay. We're going to explore a variety of music genres. Don't ask what that last word means. You'll figure it out. Who can give me a music category?"

Eyes lit up. Most had already figured out the meaning of *genre*.

"Blues."

"Okay, but too easy since we already started with that—though some of you new kids wouldn't know. Another?"

"Hip hop!" "Rock!" "Folk!" and more.

"We'll explore each of these, but I'm setting a few rules. All lyrics must be written out. Each group has to choose a scribe. No swear words. No put-downs of anyone or any group."

"You mean we can't say what bitches girls are?"

"I realize I'm throttling your creativity, but yes—you've got it right. Now let's get started."

I realized I'd become a combination English teacher and therapist. It was apparent—mostly through the Blues lyrics—that some of these kids lived incredibly difficult lives: a drunken parent, a murdered brother, no adult supervision... the list went on. I had no idea. You certainly don't learn this in a university education department.

I began to realize that most teachers came from college-educated parents, or from homes where, even if the adults hadn't gone beyond high school, education and achievement were still valued. I wondered if anyone on our faculty had ever led a life as fraught as the lives these kids were living.

When a group couldn't work out a problem with their music or lyrics, we'd talk through it. I realized some students had no concept of options. They lived in a world with limited choices—or no choices at all. What *are* the options if there's no money for food? Or if your dad comes home drunk and beats your mom or little sister?

We discussed reactions to issues and how there were always *options*. They might not be good ones. In fact, there might not be a good solution. But you had to at least look for one.

Sometimes, we discussed—either in groups or privately—how or why they'd been kicked out of class. Some were obvious: They acted inappropriately and faced the consequences. But other times, I wondered if the teacher might have handled things with more finesse.

These were teenagers, not adults. Their emotions ran high and close to the surface. Diffusing is often a better response than confrontation.

One of the boys, Ray, couldn't read any word longer than three letters. He had great ideas for lyrics, but someone else had to transcribe them. Even then, he couldn't read them back easily. One morning, Ray told me his birthday was the next day, and he thought his mom might be getting him a bicycle. I knew she had a good job, so it seemed like a possibility.

When Ray came into study hall the next day, I asked if he'd gotten the bike. He shuffled, avoided eye contact, and finally muttered, "Mom forgot it was my birthday."

I seethed inside. It wasn't like she wasn't there when he was born! How could a mother forget her son's birthday?

The next day, he didn't come to class. Nor the day after. I stopped by the office to ask if he was sick or if something else had happened. I was told he'd been suspended due to an incident in his history class.

I found his teacher, Mr. Jones, after school and asked what had happened.

"He swore at me in class. So, of course, I had to kick him out!"

Swearing was #8 on our posted list of offenses that would get you suspended. I was baffled. It didn't sound like the Ray I knew.

"I'm surprised," I said. "That doesn't sound like Ray. Why did he swear at you?"

"Once a week, I have the kids stand and read a paragraph from the text. Kind of lazy on my part, but it gives me a chance to grade papers while they drone on."

I withheld comment, though I was burning inside. "And?"

"There was an obvious lull when it was Ray's turn. I asked him to please stand and read. He just sat there, refusing to respond or look at me. I don't tolerate insubordination, so I got up from my desk and walked over. I said, 'You will stand up, and you will read.' Ray replied, 'No, I won't, you son of a bitch.' Naturally, he was sent to the office—and then home for the week."

I've never understood how suspension is considered a disciplinary tool. For many kids, getting kicked out of school is a reward—a week at home watching TV and playing video games. And if the parents work, there's no supervision at all.

I was furious with Mr. Jones for being completely clueless about Ray's reading difficulties. And there was nothing I could do. His mother transferred him to another school, and I lost track of him. There were so many tracks to try and keep up with.

Another boy, Juan, had been kicked out of math for mouthing off. He couldn't do the simplest problems, and when the teacher bawled him out, he responded rudely, and was sent to study hall. While working with rhythm and body percussion, I noticed he was struggling. He seemed to have no concept of numbers, like understanding that two is greater than one. No wonder he was having problems in math.

Before my study hall assignment, I had been teaching *music*. Now, I was teaching *kids*. And it felt so much more important.

Of course, that would have to end. And it did—almost.

"Mrs. Gilroy! Once again, you seem to have a total inability to understand your teaching assignment! I understand you have somehow turned your study hall into a music class. This will stop immediately. I'll be doing frequent checks to ensure you have resumed monitoring students. When I drop by your classroom—and trust me, I will frequently—I expect to see every student in a seat with study materials in plain sight!"

A very cooperative secretary in the office promised to text me anytime Roach left his office to prowl. Those wonderful, sneaky, "uncontrollable" kids came up with a solution.

"Mrs. Gilroy, we can figure this out. You're used to obeying rules— we spend our lives figuring out how to get around them. Every kid will always have some kind of paper or book on their desk. Only half of us can be in the practice rooms at a time, so when you get a text alert, we'll be back in our seats fast and look like we're really studying."

If you want to commit a crime, best ask a criminal how to do it. So, while it wasn't as good as before, it was far better than nothing.

CHAPTER 24

ALMOST FINISHED

Working with Jack as the house was being gutted and rebuilt was surprisingly easy. I'd heard plenty of horror stories about contractors, but Jack was always calm, professional, and made the job feel manageable. Our relationship stayed friendly but formal. The more we worked together, the more I appreciated his low-key way of managing his workers and handling any problems that arose.

Any time I came to the house to inspect the progress, he would take my arm in potentially dangerous situations—missing floor planks, rickety ladders, whatever the hazard was. I usually drove up Saturday mornings to discuss plans and check in. Once the lighting was installed, I sometimes came up on Friday evenings with a picnic dinner so we could go over the details more casually.

There was no doubt I was attracted to him. When he took my arm to steady me, I felt a definite tingle. I found myself daydreaming about him once I was back in Winston and had to take firm control of my emotions. I knew I was lonely and horny, and that combination can lead to some really stupid behavior.

A couple of guys on the faculty—one single, one married—had made it clear they were available. I might have taken the single one up on his offer, but I've always believed that having an affair with a co-worker rarely ends well. More importantly, I really didn't have the time. Still, I began to wonder if, once the project was finished, Jack and I might start a different kind of relationship. I caught him looking at me sometimes as if he were speculating, and at other times with what looked very much like desire.

To celebrate the completion of the house, he convinced me to go climbing with him one Sunday afternoon. I surprised myself by being fairly comfortable using just my hands and feet to scale a large erratic in Yosemite Valley. Oddly, it reminded me a bit of ballet—every move, every position, mattered.

After we tried a few large boulders, we took a short trail up, and he showed me how to rappel off the face of a cliff about 75 feet high. He carefully walked me through each step until I had it all down. The hardest part was coming to the edge and stepping off—backwards. Your feet do the balancing as you thread the rope, moving as slowly or as quickly as you feel safe.

I loved it. He told me it was actually the most dangerous part of climbing. Hard to believe. It was *way* fun.

As we headed back to Yosemite West, I asked, "Now that the house is finished, do you have another job lined up?"

His reply shocked me. "To quote a good old country song, *I'm movin' on*. I'm heading back to my hometown in New Hampshire. I miss my family. My dad passed a few years ago, but my mom's still there, and I've got cousins and old friends in the area. I can do contracting just as easily there—and I might teach part-time at a nearby junior college."

I was as close to speechless as I've ever been. I had grown to really like this man, and suddenly, I felt deserted.

By the time we got back to the house, it was almost dark. I threw together some appetizers, and we had a couple of beers. I *thought* it was just two beers, but what happened next made me wonder if we were a little drunk.

As he was leaving, he leaned down to give me a light kiss, which suddenly turned into much more. I don't think either of us was really thinking. Somehow, we ended up on the floor, grappling with each other's clothes, frantic with desire. The floor was uncomfortable, but thankfully, the only piece of "furniture" nearby was my sleeping bag on an air pad.

I'm not even sure I'd call what happened "lovemaking." It was so frantic it felt closer to mutual rape—except I loved it. I was sure he felt the same... but instead of lingering, he jumped up and said he had to leave.

And he did. He left.

Totally.

Gone—not just from my arms, or my house, or Yosemite—but all the way back to New Hampshire.

I thought about that crazy evening a lot. The sex had been both violent and tender at the same time, if that's even possible. Despite all my years with Jackass, I had never experienced sex like that. And Jackass had been really good in bed. Now I realized that his skill might have been honed by lots of practice.

I called it his "out-of-town tryouts."

CHAPTER 25

ELIMINATING ROACH

Now that the house was finished, I felt I'd be ready to open for business by mid-July. I had done lots of research about how to go about booking reservations. There were numerous agencies that offered those services —for a fee, of course. Each one had its own specific rules, most of which didn't work well for a small bed and breakfast like mine.

I hired a website designer, and the site would be ready to go as soon as I got some furniture in place. I was still unsure whether I should try doing everything myself or go with a company and live with their limitations. I figured I'd try to book guests daily through August 25, when I'd need to return to the classroom. After that, I'd try for two weekends per month.

It was going to be a logistical issue. I couldn't get there from my job until about 6:00 p.m., so I planned to hire a local girl to check guests in between 4:00 and 6:00. Then, on Sundays, I could start cleaning as soon as the guests checked out at 11:00 and leave for Winston around 4:00. I planned to put my Winston home on the market in a year or two and move to the mountains permanently in two or three years. I would have loved to do it that year, but I really needed the income from teaching— and I also wanted to be sure I was choosing the right path for my future.

I had only three weeks left of school, and those were always the easy weeks for me. My various singing groups had already finished their performances, and once again, they'd done a great job. Things were going well.

And then Roach called me into his office.

He'd heard rumors that I was still conducting "study hall." For a teacher, I was apparently a pretty slow learner. The kids had done so well, they wanted to perform in the talent show in early June. I figured he'd be pleased to see the Zeros so involved.

Like I said—slow learner.

"Mrs. Gilroy, you have deliberately disobeyed an order! I don't care that these losers think they're good enough to be in our talent show. That isn't going to happen. Furthermore, I see that once again you didn't win the Spring Music Festival as I directed you to do! Did you not understand that it's *WIN for Winston!*"

There didn't seem to be any point in explaining myself again. I felt like a kid being sent to the principal's office for punishment.

"I told you that if you didn't do better this semester, I'd transfer you. Here is the paperwork. Fill it out and return it to me by tomorrow."

I hated myself because, once again, I started to cry. I felt totally defeated. Then Roach surprised me by handing me a tissue and saying, "I didn't mean to be so harsh. I'm sorry. I'm having a hard time right now. My wife and I are having issues. I guess you can relate—you're divorced, right?"

Well, that was a shock. He was actually human.

I mumbled something about how these were difficult times and said I hoped he and his wife would be okay.

"Actually, she moved out two weeks ago, and I'm really lonely. I feel kind of lost at night. Why don't you bring the paperwork to my house tonight, and we can go over it over a glass of wine or two? I think you'll find that if you're willing to help me out—you know, a man has certain needs, and I'm guessing you do too—we can probably work something out. You catch my drift? And then, well, I think the transfer can be reconsidered."

"Am I hearing you correctly? If I have sex with you, you won't transfer me?"

"You don't need to be so blunt about it. We'll just kind of see how things go. You can keep your job, and I'll be a happier man."

"FUCK YOU, YOU CLUELESS SON OF A BITCH!"

I screamed it at full volume as I threw the papers at him and tore out of the room. From the looks on the office staff's faces, they'd heard every word. I ran to my car, fumbling with my keys, forgetting how to start the engine—I just knew I had to get off campus before he came after me.

I drove home in a daze and collapsed on my bed.

I had just thrown away my job—my career, my livelihood. Why hadn't I kept my head? I started going over all the clever, cool things I *could* have said instead of what I *did* say.

About an hour into my hysterics, there was a knock on the door. Thank God, it was Lori. I really needed a friend right then. She told me she'd called our union rep, Stuart, and that he was on his way over.

Even in hysteria, I was still a woman. I glanced in the mirror at the wreck of my face, grabbed a washcloth soaked in cold water, brushed my hair a little, and dabbed on some lipstick—just as Stuart arrived. I thought I was ready to have a calm conversation. Instead, I fell apart.

He just kept repeating, "It's okay. Your job is safe. You're going to be all right."

Eventually, it started to sink in.

He asked me to walk him through what had happened, and I did my best, filling him in on all the other issues I'd had with Roach too.

"I'm telling you again—your job is safe. You will not be fired. You don't have to go back for the last three weeks unless you want to. You'll still get paid."

I was floored. That was *not* what I had expected to hear.

But I still had to think about the next school year. There was only one other high school in town, though there were several more in the county. Stuart thought I should transfer and couldn't understand why I'd even *consider* working in the same building as Roach.

"What about his propositioning me?" I asked. "Can't he be fired for that?"

"Realistically? No. It becomes a he-said, she-said situation. Unless someone actually overheard him, you won't be able to prove it. Trying to pursue it would get really messy—and you probably wouldn't win."

After going over the options again and talking with Lori, I realized there was no way I could finish the year under Roach. My performances were done. He'd destroyed my study hall. And I couldn't think of a single reason to stay.

I asked Stuart to make any necessary arrangements. I was curious what excuse would be given for my sudden disappearance, but he told me not to worry.

"The word is that you developed an illness over the weekend and are unable to return this year."

After he left, Lori and I got a bit drunk on wine and expectations. I figured that despite my many years of teaching, if I were transferred, I'd be the "new teacher." Or if my seniority were honored, I'd be resented by the other teachers.

Also, Winston was part of a countywide school district. That meant I could be transferred and face a fifty-mile commute each day.

But—I needed the money.

Lori pointed out that I could sell my house and start the business earlier. Another plus: I'd have time to order and receive furniture.

Maybe Christmas came early that year.

CHAPTER 26

FURNITURE

After getting my head back on straight—and mentally sending Roach to the deepest level of Hell—I spent the rest of May and June getting the house ready. Aside from the mattresses, the furnishing process went surprisingly well. I visited furniture stores in Fresno and Oakhurst and did a lot of shopping online. Since everything had to be delivered, unpacked, and hauled inside, I enlisted help from some local folks.

Now, the mattresses... they were a story all on their own.

I had ordered four mattresses and box springs from a company my neighbor, Karen, had recommended. Before I even had the chance to unwrap them and get help moving them in, I got a phone call from the company. Another "Millie"—squeaky-voiced and apparently squeaky-brained.

"Mrs. Gilroy, you should probably check the mattresses before you bring them into the house."

"Check them for what?"

"Uh, mice?"

"You shipped me mattresses with mice?"

"Well, we discovered the problem with the next shipment, so we're not sure about yours. Please check to see if the plastic coverings have been torn and if there's any damage to the mattress itself."

"And if there is, I assume you'll replace the damaged pieces and haul them away?"

"Not really. You see, we're closing our factory."

CLICK.

Well, crap.

Sure enough, two of the mattresses had signs of mice. I found another company that agreed to haul away any damaged ones when they delivered the new set. It cost me a week's delay, but since I decided I wasn't going to pay for *any* of the original mattresses—including the two that weren't damaged—I actually saved a bit of money.

The rooms were starting to look really great, and I found myself wishing Jack were here to see how everything had turned out. But there was no word from him, and his phone no longer worked. I *tried*. It took me several days to work up the nerve to dial his cell.

"The number you have dialed is no longer in service."

So, I threw myself into making the house a perfect home—and an amazing B&B.

My kitchen was a dream. I'd spent a lot of time thinking about how I move in a kitchen—where I like appliances to be, how far apart the counters should sit, where to store table service, and where to put the pantry. Everything was built just for me. There was a double sink—much larger than standard—so a 10x15 pan could sit flat on the bottom. If I burned something, I could soak it right there. Two dishwashers flanked the sinks. There was an island with another small sink for prep work, and the island itself was butcher block—an entire cutting surface.

The range faced the dining room, but a low wall separated the spaces, so my cooking wasn't *completely* on display. Still, I could chat with guests while prepping meals. On the dining room side of that wall was a counter where the coffee and tea setup lived. The dining and living areas were essentially one large room, with windows and sliding doors opening out to the deck.

I was so in love with this place.

My bedroom was located to the right of the living area, on the north side of the house, and also faced the creek. It was spacious and cozy, with a small work area, though my main office was downstairs. My large bathroom was tucked behind the bedroom.

At the back of the house, between the kitchen and my bedroom, we designed a "den." It provided an extra sleeping space for visiting friends or family without exceeding the four-bedroom limit set by the county. Since regulations allowed only four official bedrooms, this was technically a study, outfitted with a sofa bed and double doors that could close it off from the main living area. It shared a wall with my bathroom but had its own bath entrance to satisfy the building department's guest-access requirement. There was even a small TV installed in the den in case any guests felt deprived while they were upstairs.

I was ready for business. The first guests were due to arrive next week, and I was genuinely excited.

And then I got a phone call that completely threw me off balance.

CHAPTER 27

REVIEW

A neighbor called.

"Just wondering if you're open yet."

"No, not yet," I said. "July 1. Why do you ask?"

"You know I spend quite a bit of time just prowling the Internet, and I ran across a very negative review of your place. I was pretty sure you hadn't opened yet, so I thought I'd better call."

"That's impossible," I said, assuming he must be mistaken. But when I went to the Skweel website, I did, indeed, find a really awful review of the Yosemite Butterfly Inn.

I couldn't believe what I was reading.

> I was greeted quite rudely when I arrived to check in. I was told I didn't have a reservation, even though I was holding the confirmation! I was shown my room rather reluctantly, perhaps because it was obvious the room hadn't been cleaned. After examining the bed and seeing that the sheets didn't appear to have been changed, I decided to leave and asked for a refund.

"I don't give refunds" was the only reply I got. Not seeing any point in trying to have a sane discussion with this owner, I decided to contest the charge with my credit card company and left to find pleasanter lodging.

I couldn't believe it. I was a week from opening my doors, and I already had this bogus review. Why? Who would do such a thing? And more importantly, how could I get it removed?

I called the company. The woman who answered sounded suspiciously like the mattress lady—a shrill, grating voice that made me wonder how she'd ever landed a job answering phones. Her name was Millie. I tried to explain what was going on.

Her response: "Nobody likes a bad review."

She said it three times. Her brain had to be as dense as her voice was shrill.

In my patient teacher voice, I explained, "*Review* means that you have previously viewed the room—and that's impossible, since I haven't opened yet."

This piece of logic was apparently too much for Millie, so I asked for a supervisor. All were "busy assisting other customers," and I was placed on hold. I held. And held. And held. I would've hung up, but I wasn't about to start over with Millie.

Finally, someone named Sherrie picked up. At least her voice quality was better, though I wasn't sure about the IQ. I explained the problem three times. Each time, she repeated that company policy was not to remove reviews.

"May I be connected to your legal department, please?" I asked, not even sure they had one.

A Mr. Hall picked up.

"I don't understand your problem," he said. "We vet all our letters of complaint, so obviously this guest must have stayed there. Why would someone write a review if they hadn't stayed?"

"I used to teach high school," I said, trying not to scream. "So, maybe it was a prank from a former student. Maybe I failed a kid years ago, and they see this as a chance to get even. I don't know. What I *do* know is that this is a brand-new business, and I wasn't even open at the time the supposed incident occurred."

There was a long pause.

Finally, something seemed to sink in. Mr. Hall clearly had an IQ at least somewhat above the company average.

"Well," he said, "while our policies are quite firm, we wish to assure all of our customers that we are fair and flexible. You are obviously quite distraught, which I often see with our female business owners, so I shall have the review removed—but only this one time, as a courtesy."

Ignoring his sexist comment about women in business, I thanked him. Not effusively—just professionally.

After all, I wasn't just in business.

I was the CEO.

Chapter 28

Grand Opening

It was July 1, and I was beyond excited. Two couples were arriving—one from Southern California and the other from somewhere in England. Both couples seemed very nice: pleasant to one another and to me, and eager to share experiences between them. They had both traveled extensively, so they had plenty to talk about. They liked their rooms, praised the views, and when they came upstairs for the wine and cheese hour, they were even more enthusiastic.

"Let's go out on the deck for the sunset and to see if there's any animal life on the trail just downhill," I suggested.

I played the generous host and poured a nice Chardonnay for the guests—and for myself.

"Since you're my very first guests, I made some special appetizers for you to sample. Please let me know which ones you think are the best. I think you'll really enjoy the *SHERRY BISCUITS* hot out of the oven—spread them with Camembert."

After our third glass of wine, I was a bit woozy, and the guests weren't sure they wanted to go out to dinner. Honestly, maybe they shouldn't have driven anyway.

Mental note: Serve fewer appetizers (I really went overboard) and control the pouring of wine rather than just putting a bottle or two out.

When I went to B&B school, I noticed some hosts served sherry in the evening. It seemed rather old-fashioned to me—or possibly a British tradition. Aside from the biscuits, I didn't even like sherry. This was California, after all, and I wanted to celebrate our wonderful wines. But I also wasn't in the wine tasting business, and drinking generous amounts of wine with guests every night didn't seem very smart. I began to understand the wisdom of sherry—though I still wouldn't serve it.

"You're my very first guests, and I hope you're enjoying yourselves," I said, standing up with a smile. "I'd stay longer, but I have lots of office work to do." *Hint, hint.* "You're welcome to use the upper floor anytime. The study's a good place to read or watch TV if your roommate wants to sleep and you're a night owl."

The next morning—only slightly hungover—I made a frittata, my go-to breakfast when I wasn't quite firing on all cylinders. I added CONFETTI MUFFINS from the freezer and a fruit platter. I felt very satisfied with myself. When the couples left after their two-night stay, they were complimentary and promised to leave a glowing review online.

I was delighted. I felt like I was born to do this business. I was a natural. It was so easy and so fun.

And then the next guests arrived... and I learned that not everything was coming up roses.

Poison ivy would be more accurate.

CHAPTER 29

HOW TO RUN A BED AND BREAKFAST (OR MAYBE NOT)

Still new at this business—actually, *very* new, since it was only my first week—I saw the car pull into the drive, so I was at the door, smiling and ready to greet my next guests. The woman practically fell out of the car in her rush to get out, though not from excitement, as it turned out.

"Welcome to the Yosemite Butterfly," I said warmly.

Her response? "I hate Yosemite."

It didn't take a psychic to forecast that things might go downhill from there. Her male companion had already removed their luggage and greeted me with a rather tight expression. By the time I showed them to their room, she had made three more complaints, and her companion looked increasingly miserable. Evidently, he'd planned this as a surprise trip to a national park—while she'd thought they were headed for Las Vegas and had packed accordingly.

There was no way Yosemite and Vegas could be confused—or compared—and no way to shut her up, so I simply went upstairs, processed a refund, and came back down with that and directions to Las Vegas. My small revenge: It was a *long, long* drive.

But things improved. After a month in business—while I was hardly an expert in running a B&B—I was learning fast. I recognized early on that the daily "grind" of creating interesting breakfasts, serving them

119

artistically, cleaning up, cleaning rooms, shopping, greeting new guests, setting out wine and cheese each evening, and being constantly available day and night could be exhausting—and would only get worse.

Needing to establish my business and really needing the income, I booked every room I could, every time I could. During the summer, that often meant seven days a week and countless hours each day. At that rate, I wasn't sure I could make it to the three-year average. The variety of guests, and their needs or outright demands, started to wear on me within a few weeks.

For instance, on the reservation form, there was a space to list any food allergies or dislikes. Few guests bothered to fill it out, but then they'd surprise me upon arrival—or at breakfast the next morning.

"Oh, sorry, I'm allergic to eggs."

"Just cooked eggs, or eggs in things like muffins?" I'd ask, trying not to grind my teeth while thinking sarcastically, *Eggs! Who would ever think to serve* those *at breakfast?*

Usually, it turned out to be more of a trauma than an allergy—often tied to some childhood memory of being forced to eat fried eggs. One guest even told me how, when she was about twelve, she refused to eat her breakfast egg. When she came home from school, she found it sitting on the walkway to her house—and her mother made her get down on her hands and knees and eat the egg off the sidewalk.

I could hardly blame her for never wanting to see another fried egg again.

So, when I served eggs, I scrambled or baked them. If I poached or fried them, I disguised them. One of my favorites was PEREGRINE EGGS, named after the peregrine falcons that had once been endangered until major efforts were made to save them from extinction.

Even though DDT had been banned in the U.S. since 1972, it was still widely used in Mexico. During their winter migration, peregrines fed on local birds in Mexico that had eaten contaminated food. When the falcons returned to Yosemite and nested high up on ledges on El Capitan, the DDT made their eggshells so fragile that they cracked under the weight of the nesting parents.

An ambitious project in Santa Cruz was launched to save the species. When the peregrines returned in spring to nest, climbers scaled

El Capitan, replaced the real eggs with ceramic fakes, and took the fragile real ones to Santa Cruz to be incubated. The chicks were fed using bird hand puppets and, once old enough, were returned to the nests in Yosemite. The falcon parents accepted them without hesitation and resumed their hunting, feeding the chicks through regurgitation.

Peregrines are picky eaters. Unlike other birds of prey, they don't eat carrion off the ground. They work as a team, performing a complex aerial ballet—a *pas de deux*. One falcon flies through a flock to startle them, making them less watchful. The second falcon dives from above to catch an unsuspecting bird mid-flight. Peregrines have been clocked at over 200 miles per hour. I once watched a pair attempt this on a flock of ravens, but ravens are incredibly smart and seemed to catch on. They reversed the game and began attacking the peregrines. Luckily, the falcons were faster, but I suspect they gave ravens a wide berth after that.

For Peregrine Eggs, I toasted half an English muffin, topped it with a poached egg, and decorated it: wings made from half-slices of fried porcini mushrooms, a tail fashioned from a sliced mushroom fanned out, a sausage-slice "head," and a small triangle of yellow pepper for a beak. I spooned on a bit of mushroom gravy mixed with sour cream to disguise the egg. Never a single complaint!

There were other food issues, too. One woman who stayed for five days informed me *after* arrival that she was gluten intolerant. That threw me into a scramble. I wasn't a short-order cook, so I had to accommodate her without sacrificing meals for everyone else. I served things like polenta, corn pancakes, and rice puddings. It was a stretch.

On her last day, just before checking out, she smiled and said, "Thanks for all your efforts. I was really just experimenting to see if I was allergic—but evidently, I'm not!"

I refrained from throwing something at her. Or screaming.

Lesson learned: When someone claims a food allergy, it might just be a strong dislike. But it's also a chance to show them that something they've always avoided might become a new favorite—if prepared with care and creativity.

CHAPTER 30

SOLVING FOOD ISSUES

"So how do you cook for foreign guests whose breakfasts are often so different from American ones?" A frequent question from friends or other guests.

If it was just one couple out of the three rooms who were from another country, I tried to incorporate familiar flavors or names, like I had with my venture into *Yorkshire pudding,* better known in America as *Dutch Baby*. Once, I had three Italian couples visiting at the same time. They spoke about as much English as I did Italian—in other words, fewer than ten words.

I had been to Italy, and I knew that as you traveled farther south in Europe, breakfasts tended to become sparser and lighter. In Finland, a hotel might lay out a lavish buffet that filled two rooms. In France, you were lucky to get a croissant and coffee. In Italy, it might be just a crust of bread and an espresso.

So, for these Italians, I created ALMOND FRENCH TOAST. I sliced a loaf of crusty French bread and soaked it in a milk and egg mixture seasoned with almond extract, then fried the slices in butter until they were golden brown. I presented a full platter of what I called "Italian-style French toast," topping the slices with lemon curd and toasted, slivered almonds. I served fresh fruit on the side—and ended up with some very happy Italians.

The three Chinese couples who came later were a bit more of a challenge. I didn't often get Asian guests, as they typically traveled through agencies, just as Americans tend to do when visiting foreign countries. It makes the trip easier: no language barrier, and all your needs are handled by the tour group.

But these couples were traveling independently and seemed very comfortable doing so. Two of the men had worked with their foreign office in the U.S. and spoke excellent English, translating for their wives and the other couple. The challenge was what to serve them during their weekend stay.

I decided to serve a typical Chinese breakfast one morning and a traditional American breakfast the next.

CONGEE was my choice for the Chinese meal. Sometimes called "juk" in Chinese households, it's a dish that surprises most Americans when I tell them about it.

When I shared this story with friends, their response was always the same: "Congee? Never heard of it."

I'd reply, "Think of it as the culinary version of the biblical loaves and fishes—where Christ fed the multitudes. You start with almost nothing and end up with more than you'll ever need."

It was simple to make. I just cooked rice in chicken broth... *forever*. In America, we're used to perfectly fluffy rice in 20 minutes: two cups of water, one cup of rice, done. Not with congee. It's unlimited broth and what seems like unlimited cooking time. The longer it cooked, the more it expanded. I was sure there had to be a limit to its growth, but I hadn't found it yet.

The first time I made it, I started at 6:00 a.m. with a cup of rice and just kept adding broth. I lost count of how much I poured in, but by 8:00 a.m., I had far more than I needed for six people. It had the consistency of a thick, goopy cereal.

I added some diced vegetables—carrots and bell peppers—a bit of mild crumbled sausage, and seasoned it with soy sauce. Toward the end, I tossed in frozen peas and chopped green onions. Just before serving, I scooped it into deep bowls and cracked a fresh egg into the hot congee, letting the heat cook it gently until the yolk was just soft.

The guests were delighted with my attempt, though I'm sure it wasn't perfectly authentic.

Another food issue I hadn't anticipated was late arrivals. Guests would show up late and then ask, "Where can we get dinner?" My B&B was thirty minutes from the nearest restaurants—either in Yosemite Valley or Wawona—and neither of them served past 9:00 p.m.

Even though I was very clear about check-in times, travel delays happened. I quickly learned to warn guests driving in from San Francisco to expect heavy commuter traffic after 3:30 p.m.

Eventually, I started stocking a few prepackaged meals in the freezer. Guests could use the microwave downstairs in the laundry area if they needed something after hours. It was a simple solution, but I had to learn it the hard way.

Before I thought of that fix, I had two late-arriving couples back-to-back, and I had to scramble to throw together some kind of dinner from the supplies I had on hand.

Making dinner *and* breakfast? Definitely too much.

CHAPTER 31

YOSEMITE WILDLIFE

Practically everyone who comes to Yosemite knows there are bears here. I'd say *wild* bears, but they've become so accustomed to people that I'm not sure it's still accurate. Years ago, the Park Service used to dump garbage into an open trench, and tourists would come just to watch the bears feed. Eventually, it became clear that this was basically training the bears to eat human food, so the garbage ritual was ended. But the bears didn't forget. They passed that knowledge on to their cubs—just like humans do. Even the young ones now seem to know that human food is delicious... and often easy to get.

I once had a bear come into the house through a door I'd left ajar for just a few minutes while I was serving breakfast on the deck.

"What did you do?" guests always asked.

"I told him to leave, of course!" That line never failed to raise eyebrows.

"Okay," I'd confess. "I used to teach high school, so I have a voice of authority."

Thankfully, the bear did leave. I'm not sure what I would've done if he hadn't. After that incident, I bought some pepper spray—but so far, I haven't had to use it.

When my neighbor Al is around, I always ask him to tell guests about "Curious George" and his visit. Al is a natural storyteller, and this one never fails to delight.

"This bear had been checking out our upper deck for the past two days," he'd begin. "My wife and I were getting ready to go out of town, and we got a bit worried. I figured the bear had climbed the large ponderosa just off the deck, so I had it cut down to discourage any further visits. Not cheap, by the way!"

I'd add, for the guests' understanding, that Al's house, like mine, was on a slope—so his deck was actually three stories up.

Al continued, "Apparently, I didn't think things through very well. That damned bear—pardon my swearing, ladies—got back on the deck anyway. Must've climbed the support posts. Then, when he couldn't get in through the doors, he climbed up onto the railing and somehow reached around to the kitchen window—a sliding window we forgot to lock. He's three stories off the ground, leaning out into thin air to open that window. It's a hell of a stretch—pardon me again."

The guests always gasped, picturing the bear stretched out, suspended over nothing.

"Somehow, he did a Tarzan move and made it through the window. Didn't even break it. And he was well rewarded. He did a thorough sweep of the kitchen—*thorough*! Every package, every can, out of the cupboards and onto the floor for inspection."

Gasps all around.

"But he wasn't done. Everything in the fridge and freezer came out, too. And yes, he found some favorites—cocoa powder and olive oil. We know that because he tracked them on his paws all over the rest of the house."

We all imagined what those floors and carpets must have looked like.

"But George was a clean bear," Al said with a grin. "He went downstairs and decided to take a shower. Problem is, he forgot to close the shower door and turn the water off. Luckily, being on the lower level, it didn't flood the rest of the house. Unluckily, he locked himself in the bathroom. He took down the light fixtures, trying to get out, but that didn't help. Then he started peeling off some drywall, but the studs were too close together to squeeze through. Eventually, he figured out the door. It was a cheap hollow-core door—just cardboard in the middle. He busted through that and was long gone by the time we got back."

Everyone's jaws were usually on the floor at this point—even mine, and I'd heard the story before. Like the guests, I was imagining how I would've reacted if it had been *my* kitchen and *my* flooded bathroom.

I always joked with Al at the end, "Well, at least the rangers didn't cite you for feeding the wildlife!"

I never tried to top his story, but the questions from guests continued—mostly about other animals.

Once in a while, I'd get, "When do they let the bears out?"

They are always out.

Most people come from cities, so I understand the disconnect. In the city, wild animals are safely behind glass or fences at zoos. Insects and rodents are something to be exterminated. Everything has a place. But Yosemite isn't the city. Here, animals live as they please—free to wander, hunt, and multiply.

"Yes," I would tell them, "That odd creature in your sink is a scorpion. I'll take care of it. Their sting is unpleasant but rarely dangerous."

Spiders? Yes, we have plenty. Some small, some the size of your hand. Wolf spiders and tarantulas are the largest. I've learned to trap them and release them outside—where I hope they'll stay.

"No, I don't kill spiders," I'd add, often to raised eyebrows.

Snakes? We have a few. Most are shy and keep their distance. If I see a rattlesnake near the house that refuses to leave, I kill it with a shovel blade behind the neck. But I much prefer to scare them off with loud noises and a stick.

Rodents? Absolutely. Mice love the warmth of guest rooms in winter. Ground squirrels, tree squirrels, and even flying squirrels, which you can sometimes see from the upper deck. Occasionally, one gets into the walls or ceilings, and then I have to live with the noise until I figure out how to lure it out.

"You say you have some very large ants walking through your room?" I'd ask. "Well, I'll come down and watch them with you if you'd like."

Unlike the tiny sugar ants, carpenter ants just kind of wander about, possibly doing structural damage. I find them disturbing, but also strangely aimless. They usually disappear after a few hours.

The howling at night? Coyotes, of course. Usually at 5:00 a.m.—and yes, it's annoying. One of many reasons I don't allow pets. Guests arrive with little Fifi, and then, realizing dogs aren't allowed on the trails, they want to leave her on the deck for the day. For coyotes—who somehow manage to reach even high decks—that's just a lovely afternoon snack.

And yes, there are lynx and mountain lions around. Stories about lions attacking people always make the news and stir up fear, but in reality, I've only seen a mountain lion once, and that was in a very remote part of the park. I spotted a lynx once on the Yosemite Falls Trail. I hike and ski alone often and never feel unsafe. I know there is at least one cougar nearby, but it has never shown itself to me.

So, no, it isn't a zoo or an animal park. We do our best to keep the wildlife *wild*. You can be here for a week or more and never see any of it, so really, there is no point in worrying.

CHAPTER 32

DIFFICULT GUESTS AND MORE FOOD ISSUES

Friends always ask, "How do you deal with difficult guests?"

"There really aren't too many," I reply. "Most guests truly love Yosemite and appreciate being in a more intimate setting than a motel." But because there were so few difficult ones, they became memorable. The best advice I got from an experienced innkeeper was, "Give them their money back right at the first complaint, and you'll be happier in the end."

It took time to really grasp the reality that some guests are never going to be happy, and their very presence can ruin the experience for everyone else. Some situations are relatively easy, like the woman who arrived absolutely terrified. Her boyfriend had driven the mountain roads—those spectacular ones with sheer drop-offs and no rails, and she had spent the entire drive lying on the floor of the car with a blanket over her head. She arrived distraught and carsick. As soon as they were settled in their room, I brought her some hot tea and suggested a soak in the hot tub. Her equilibrium was restored enough to join the others for wine hour.

Another time, I had shown a couple to their room, and the woman immediately began a major inspection.

"This bedspread is dirty and will have to be replaced."

"It was just washed before your arrival," I said. "What you're pointing out—that small area on the printed fabric—is where the dye has run slightly out of the outline."

"That is clearly dirt and I insist on a new bed covering!"

So, I went up to the attic and brought down a replacement. By the time I returned, she was already complaining about the plastic glasses on the sideboard.

"Those are for the hot tub," I explained. "There are stemmed wine glasses and glass tumblers on the shelf."

"On a shelf? Then they're no doubt dusty. I don't drink from plastic," she sniffed.

At that point, I recognized a no-win situation. Much as I hated giving refunds—especially since I was too far off the highway for someone else to stumble upon me last-minute—there was a bit of sweet revenge in giving them their money back. There was no way they'd find another room nearby. Most Yosemite West lodging was entire-home rentals, and the only other B&B was perpetually booked. They'd likely have to drive back out of the park—probably to Oakhurst, an hour south—and then sit in line for another hour the next morning to get back in. I smiled as I handed them their refund.

Food issues for one person while cooking for six are never easy. For vegetarians, my go-to is BREAKFAST FAJITAS—scrambled eggs in corn tortillas with all the toppings placed on a lazy Susan in the center of the table. For vegans, I scramble tofu instead. But I hadn't found other great ways to serve one vegan while accommodating five other guests, so I eventually stopped trying.

My favorite example of difficult guests? *The honeymooners.*

Certain things bring universal joy—a new baby, a beautiful sunset, and newlyweds. I always look forward to honeymooners. They are so cute in the way they look at each other and seem to forget anyone else is around. This couple was no exception. When I showed them to their room, they could barely wait for me to leave. I made sure to remind them—twice—that breakfast would be served at 8:30 in case they got... distracted.

"For breakfast, I'll be making my specialty: *Honeymoon Biscuits,*" I told them.

I called them that because I added pepper to the dough—after all, a marriage should have a bit of spice. What most people didn't know was that you could make biscuit or scone dough ahead of time, shape it, freeze it, and then bake as usual. Maybe just add a couple of minutes.

The next morning, 8:30 rolled around and four of my six guests arrived. The honeymooners didn't. We waited a few more minutes, then I served breakfast. The other guests were checking out that day, so after breakfast, they packed up and left. Still no sign of the honeymooners. Thankfully, I had soundproofed the rooms well.

By noon—with still no appearance—I left a note and headed out for groceries, hoping to see them at the evening wine hour.

Nope. Another no-show.

That evening, I had a couple of local friends over for dinner. After the new guests left to eat, we took over my kitchen and began prepping a stir fry. One friend was making egg rolls from scratch. The counters were covered in vegetables and bowls when suddenly—there they were. The honeymooners. Loaded with groceries.

"We need to use your kitchen. Now."

"What?" I said, stunned. "As you can see, the kitchen is already in use. And I don't allow guests to use it. It's actually against county rules for a B&B to let guests cook—it's considered a safety and liability issue." (I wasn't sure if that was true, but it sounded good.)

"What are we supposed to do? We have steaks, potatoes to bake, broccoli, and dessert."

"You're welcome to use the barbecue for the steaks, and the microwave downstairs for the rest."

That clearly wasn't what they wanted. As they huffed away, I heard the man mutter, "Some honeymoon, when she can't even handle a simple problem."

They didn't show for breakfast the next morning either. When I went down to check, I found they had already left. The note in my guest book said it all:

This so-called bed and breakfast didn't even serve

*breakfast. And the owner was totally unable to accommo-
date a simple request. We'll be writing a review for
Skweel.*

They also mentioned how kindly they'd been treated at the previous place they stayed. Curious, I called the Green Parrot in Santa Barbara. I only had to say "honeymooners" before the owner groaned.

"Worst guests we've ever had! Stayed two nights—totally demanding and rude. Wanted breakfast at a different time than we served, expected to use our kitchen, wanted to park in our garage instead of the guest lot..."

I hoped that was the last of that "happy couple." But as promised, they left a review on Skweel.

When you get a negative review, it's hard to know whether to respond or ignore it. I decided to ignore that one. But a few months later, I received a handwritten note from three couples from Ireland as they were checking out. It listed several ridiculous allegations—dirty dishes, unclean sheets, no breakfast—and ended with:

*If you don't give us our money back, we will send
out very negative reviews.*

Sure enough, one of them did.

This time, I scanned the note and sent it in response to the review with the comment: "I believe this is called blackmail. I chose not to refund money to this person or his friends."

CHAPTER 33

THE MOST FOREIGN GUEST

It's early November, and since no one seems interested in coming to the B&B, I block out the three-day Armistice weekend and agree to meet Lori in Fresno. We leave her car there and head for the North Coast—Mendocino, specifically. It's a long day of driving, which we split between us, and we arrive at a B&B in Mendocino around 7:00 p.m.

On Sunday, we explore the local area and both agree we need to come up here more often. Our jobs are definitely interfering with our fun. We drive farther north, up through the coastal redwoods, and spot some redwood and driftwood creations on the side of the highway. Most of it is the usual tourist bait—ugly things like a thousand identical redwood windmills—but one beautifully carved redwood bench catches our attention. So did a metal and driftwood waterfall sculpture that would look amazing on my deck.

I talk to the creator—a tall, lanky Southerner who introduces himself as John Smith. I can't help but wonder what his name was last week, but I figure it's none of my business. Lori and I agree the waterfall is truly a work of art, and the price is surprisingly reasonable. The problem? It's too big to fit in my car.

John nods knowingly. "Yup. Everybody admires my stuff, but nobody buys it. Too big to haul. Where y'all live?"

"Yosemite."

"You buy it, I'll haul it for gas money. I ain't never been to Yosemite."

"Tell you what," I say, "It's at least an eight-hour drive to my place, but if you're willing to make the trip, I can put you up for the night."

"You got yourself a deal, lady. Ain't nobody here buyin' stuff anyway."

I pay by credit card, silently hoping I won't have to dispute the charge if he never shows up. Then Lori and I drive partway back, stopping in Santa Rosa for the night.

A couple of days later, he calls. He's coming this weekend. And, to my surprise, he actually shows up—waterfall and bench in tow. He also brings a passenger: A woman he introduces as his wife. Her name is Sunny, which stands in stark contrast to her appearance. She looks like she's stepped out of the deep backwoods of Appalachia—places so dense with trees, she's maybe never seen the sun.

She's the color of a mushroom, painfully thin, with shoulder-length, stringy hair in need of a good wash. Her dress, a simple shift the same dull shade as her skin, is far too light for the November chill.

John grunts a thank-you when I show them their room, but Sunny just stands there, wide-eyed. "I ain't never seen anything as purty as this," she whispers.

Later, after the other guests leave for dinner, they come upstairs.

"Would you like me to tell you about the special places in Yosemite Valley?" I ask. "You could get dinner there, too."

John answers for both of them. "No ma'am. We didn't plan to go out for dinner. We're kinda tired."

There is some awkward shifting between them, and it dawns on me that they probably don't have the money to eat out.

"Well," I say, "Would you like to have dinner with me? I usually eat alone, and I'd enjoy your company."

They exchange looks again. John finally mutters, "That's mighty nice of you. But we don't eat too many things... don't like salad stuff. And we don't eat fish."

Living next to some of the best fishing grounds in the country and they don't like fish!

"You're in luck," I smile. "I made a nice pot of stew, and I'll bake some biscuits to go with it."

Both the stew and the biscuits are a hit, at least based on John's approving nods. He clearly prefers to do the talking (and the nodding) for both of them.

Over dinner, I try to break the silence. "Do you have any children?"

"No, ma'am. Got six by my first wife."

"Oh my. Where are they now?"

"Don't rightly know. She left me. I treated that woman so fine. Bought her a 27-inch TV. I come home one day, she's sittin' there smokin' and watchin' the TV, not payin' them kids no never mind. One of 'em even had a dirty diaper. I was so mad, I grabbed that TV—didn't unplug it or nothin'—just grabbed it real strong and threw it out the door. Said, 'You're next, bitch!' and she left me."

There really isn't much I can say to that story. I manage a weak "Well, I'll be..." and make a few sympathetic sounds, hoping they'll retire soon—which thankfully, they do.

You can imagine breakfast the next morning. The other two couples —both pretty sophisticated travelers—come up first, so I have a chance to quietly explain why my "foreign" guests are here.

I'm not sure if Sunny and John actually eat anything before fleeing back to the safety of the North Coast. The other guests, however, enjoy the BREAKFAST ROLL-UPS and fruit-filled CREPES.

Here's the roll-up recipe that saved the day:

BREAKFAST ROLL-UPS

• Three very large colored flour tortillas
• Spreadable cream cheese
• Grated cheddar/jack or Mexican blend cheese
• Baby spinach leaves
• Six eggs, whisked with the juice from half a lime and ½ tsp ground cumin
• Choice of: chopped green chiles, roasted red peppers, chorizo, cilantro

Slice about two inches off one side of each tortilla. Spread cream cheese over the surface, add a layer of spinach, and top with grated cheese. Scramble the eggs and use one-third per tortilla, placing it in a line near the cut edge. Add your choice of extras to the eggs. Roll tightly from the cut edge, trim the empty end, and when ready to serve, slice each roll into six pieces. Keep them intact under a damp paper towel and microwave for one minute. Serve three pieces per guest, with mango or pineapple on the side.

CHAPTER 34

END OF SEASON

For my first short season, I felt pretty confident—not just that I could run this business, but that I would actually enjoy it. However, every business needs income, and mine suddenly stopped. Guests had come through most of October, but then November arrived, and with it... almost no one.

I called the other B&B owner. "Karen, what's happening? Nobody is coming! Aside from Thanksgiving, I only have three other reservations for the entire month."

"Welcome to *November Nada!*" she said. "It was a harsh lesson for me two years ago when I started—and nothing's changed."

"You tried special offers or something?" I asked.

"Anything you can dream up, I tried. People just don't seem to think of traveling in November, I guess. Can't really blame them—our weather here isn't very pleasant unless you like rain. There's never any snow, or at least not enough for Badger Pass to open. And the Park Service, in keeping with their motto, has probably already closed both Tioga Pass and Glacier Point roads, so visitors are limited to Yosemite Valley."

"What motto?" I asked.

"'When it rains, it's chains. When it snows, we close.' Not *actually* their motto, of course, but you'll get as frustrated as the rest of us by how quickly they close roads. In fairness, they're trying to protect flat-landers from themselves on snowy mountain roads. There are always accidents. Plus, there are occasional rockfalls, especially on Highway 140 above El Portal."

"So, what do you do with most of November?"

"I take a vacation! I usually come back for Thanksgiving, but not always. Early December's just a repeat of November—and winter's not much better."

"I guess I've been a bit naive. I just assumed reservations would keep rolling in."

"Our business is definitely seasonal," she said, "and I haven't found any way around it. So, I make other plans."

"Thanks, Karen," I said, half grateful, half disheartened.

It looked like I'd have plenty of time to catch up on paperwork, repairs, deep cleaning... all the "fun" parts of life.

Julie planned to spend Thanksgiving Day with her dad but would come up for the rest of the weekend to help out and keep me company. Her dad was planning to spend Christmas with Giselle, so I could count on Julie being with me the whole holiday. Tommy couldn't fly out this year—he'd be spending the holidays with Gioia's family in New York—but he promised to come next year.

I called the registered guests who were due to come for the Thanksgiving and Christmas holidays.

"Since dining out in winter is more limited than in summer—and usually a bit of a drive—I'll be happy to fix dinner for you on the nights you choose, just for the cost of the food."

Some had other plans, but a few took me up on the offer. For Thanksgiving Eve, I made a hearty soup and homemade bread with a light dessert. The holiday itself got the full treatment: turkey, stuffing, the works.

Some might not think this is the ideal way to spend a holiday, but I was in my element—in the kitchen. Dinner the next day? Turkey sandwiches, of course. And for Saturday, if anyone wanted dinner again, I offered homemade turkey pot pies.

Julie arrived the week before Christmas, and we had so much fun decorating.

"Mom, what are we going to do for a tree?" she asked.

"We'll buy one this year," I said. "But next Christmas, when Tommy comes, he and Jaden can cut one from the property. Let's walk down near the bottom of the lot—I'll show you the one I have in mind."

"Wow, Mom, that's at least twelve feet tall—maybe more! It'll be fabulous!"

It was so good to have her there. She helped with cooking, too. All three couples had decided to let me make their Christmas banquet, and Julie had claimed dessert and appetizers while I handled the main dish.

We set the table for eight, since we'd be joining the guests for dinner. When I brought out the main dish, it looked like a perfectly browned roast turkey.

"Gorgeous turkey!" some of the guests said.

"But looks can be deceiving," I teased. "This is called TURKEY MOSAIC."

There were puzzled glances—except from Julie, who knew what was coming. This had been my dad's specialty, a recipe he'd clipped from *Gourmet Magazine* years ago, and she remembered it well.

I cut into the turkey, revealing a mosaic of three colors of meat held together with a green grout.

Gasps of amazement followed.

"How did you ever do that?"

"Did it take you all day?" one of the women asked.

As I served, I explained how it was done: "First, you debone the turkey, leaving the skin, wings, and drumsticks intact. Then you slice the meat about three-quarters of an inch thick. You'll also need raw chicken meat—it's pinker than turkey—and some roast ham, which is pinker still."

One of the men asked, "So what's the green stuff?"

"The grout is chopped frozen spinach—thawed and well-drained— mixed with egg and cream cheese. You layer the meats, separated by the spinach mix, and then you roast it all."

And then I added, "Yes, it takes all day. And this may be my first and last attempt!"

The women all nodded in complete understanding, but two of the men were utterly fascinated. I brought out the original, well-worn *Gourmet Magazine* with the recipe, and I could tell—this dish would be making a debut at their next family holiday.

CHAPTER 35

TEACHING SKIING

January came, and I quickly realized it was going to be *way* too quiet. Karen had warned me, but I hadn't quite internalized it until now: Business was slow, as in almost nonexistent. The B&B was booked for the occasional weekend and the Martin Luther King holiday, but almost nothing midweek. February and March weren't shaping up any better.

The consequences weren't just financial—though the reality of stretching a seven-month income across twelve months was hitting hard —they were also emotional. What was I supposed to do with all this *time*?

I decided to volunteer as a ski instructor for the two local elementary schools' PE programs. During winter, due to unpredictable weather and road conditions, regular PE was replaced with a weekly ski day, understandably popular. Teachers and community members who could ski stepped in to teach kindergarten through eighth grade. While I was primarily a cross-country skier, I was reasonably proficient in downhill —at least enough for beginners.

On my first day on the "job," I was assigned six children, mostly five- or six-year-olds, with one ten-year-old new to the school.

"Okay, kids," I began, "the first thing we're going to do is check that our boots feel okay and that our skis are attached properly."

They immediately looked down, and two of them fell over doing so. As I helped them up, the ten-year-old piped up, "Miss! How come your skis are so long and skinny?"

I smiled. "These are cross-country skis, or Nordic skis. I wear them to teach because they're better for going uphill. They're a little harder to balance on than yours, but I'll switch to downhill skis—Alpine skis—when we're ready for the bigger hills."

All eyes looked up to the slope ahead of us, which must have seemed enormous to a five-year-old. I could see the mixture of anticipation and fear.

"I promise we'll be up there in just a few weeks," I assured them, "after you've learned the basics. For now, let's go over to the rope tow."

I showed them how to grab the rope that would gently pull them to the top of a small hill. Two kids immediately fell. The operator stopped the rope, which caused two more to fall. The top of that small hill started to look farther and farther away. It was going to be a *long* morning.

Still, the reward for my efforts was a free lift ticket to use in the afternoon.

Unfortunately, mastering the rope tow was the only way to get the kids up even the slightest slope, where they could learn the basics—how to turn, and most importantly, how to stop. I had to admire the rope tow operator's patience. Together, we watched the children we'd both coached now fall off the rope in a steady rotation. That meant I had to help them get out of the path before the next kid collided with them. A sudden stop usually meant the whole line went down. My Nordic skis earned their keep in those rescue operations.

Eventually, we were all assembled at the top, and it was time for their first baby steps downhill. Despite my repeated instructions to parents not to hover, some had snuck over, cell phones out, trying to document the occasion. Naturally, the kids under parental surveillance were the first to fall—and some even started crying.

Once the parents left, the kids made real progress. They learned to wedge their skis ("make a slice of pizza") and even began turning. Toward the end of the morning, I brought them to the beginners' hill and their first ski lift ride. They picked it up far faster than the rope tow.

At the top, I reminded them again to use their snowplow technique. Despite my *very* clear instructions, I found myself rescuing kids who fell and couldn't get back up. Again, my cross-country skis let me move quickly uphill to help.

By lunchtime, I was tired—but determined to use my free pass on the bigger hills. I spent the afternoon practicing telemark turns. By 4:00, I was truly exhausted and drove home, sore but satisfied.

This—and a few cross-country ski trips—would help keep me sane through winter. Still, I wasn't sure how sustainable it was. I found myself looking forward to late March and the return of guests.

Spring and summer were booking up almost solid, and I was glad to be working hard again. I refused to think back to last spring and Jack's sudden departure. And I certainly wasn't going to dwell on what happened just before he took off. As Lori would be happy to remind me, *"So it goes."*

I was better organized than I'd been the year before, and I was perfecting my recipes. I had a handle on this, and nothing was going to spoil it.

Of course, that was *before* I met Evil Evelyn.

CHAPTER 36

JONATHAN

The day after Lori and I return from our incredible trip to the East Side, I call Jonathan to catch up—mainly to tell him about Evelyn's dramatic reappearance.

"Don't tell me over the phone," he says. "Why don't I drive up tomorrow? We can take a hike, and you can tell me in person. I'll bring lunch for both of us."

He arrives around 10:00 the next morning, and I immediately launch into the tale of my latest Evelyn conquest.

"Cool it! Save the story for our lunch break, where we can properly savor it," he says with a smile. "And I have some news about progress."

"Okay," I reply. "I'm thinking we might hike to the top of Vernal Falls, and if we're up for it, continue on to Nevada Falls."

"Great. I did that hike years ago. I'd love to do it again—with you."

That simple comment sends a little flutter through me. There is definitely a connection here—something mutual—and I am eager to explore it.

We drive down to the Valley and park at Curry Village, then walk to Happy Isles and the trailhead. The mile-long ascent to the base of Vernal Falls is gently uphill, and we chat casually as we climb. At the bridge below the falls, the trail splits. The horse trail—the longer, easier route

—branches off to the right. Though it is paved, which always feels a bit strange for a national park, I understand it is necessary to control erosion. Rangers use it to carry supplies to the backcountry, and it used to be a tourist favorite before the Valley stables were removed.

But we are taking the Mist Trail.

The trail climbs steeply along a staircase of stone, well-maintained by trail crews over the years. In late spring, with the waterfall in full force, this trail earns its name—you can get soaked without a jacket. But today, it is dry and manageable. At the top, we pause to admire the peaceful pond.

"Do people swim here in summer?" Jonathan asks.

"They do," I say, "and every year someone misjudges the current and gets swept over the falls. You'd think they'd pay attention to all the graphic warning signs, but no—someone always has to prove the signs wrong."

It is too early for lunch, so we agree to continue up to Nevada Falls. The climb is longer but dry.

"Do people go over this one, too?" he asks.

"Yeah, unfortunately. I remember—I was maybe ten, hiking with my parents, and we saw someone get swept over. It haunted me for years. I couldn't take this trail again for a long time, and I used to have nightmares. People take off their boots at the top and wade in to cool their feet, but the water's deceptively shallow, and the current is strong. All it takes is one step too far, and the sand slips out from under you... and you're gone."

"Oh, God. I'm so sorry I asked."

"It's okay. The memories have dulled with time, and I've learned to talk about it—especially with my guests. This is a popular rest stop for people hiking to Half Dome, so it's important to talk about the danger."

"Do many of your guests do that hike?"

"Now that it requires a permit, not as many. But I've had guests tell me after breakfast they're 'just going to hike Half Dome today,' not realizing it's a seventeen-mile round trip and a 5,000-foot climb. I usually offer to pack them a breakfast if they have a permit. A few still try it. Most either change their minds or only make it partway."

At the top, we find a spot by the pool and unpack our lunch. Jonathan looks at me, grinning.

"I've waited long enough. Tell me about Dear Evelyn and her latest foray, and then I'll give you a progress update on the case."

He already knows Lori and I went to the East Side to see the aspens, but he doesn't know the best part—Evelyn's failed ambush. I recount the whole thing, emphasizing Lori's quick wit and cutting commentary. Jonathan laughs and shakes his head, clearly impressed.

"Obviously, I need to meet Lori. She sounds like the best possible friend to have. As for the case... I believe 'Evelyn'—not her real name—has been involved in at least two other fraud attempts, but charges were dropped due to lack of proof. I'm reaching out to the people she tried to scam. If I can show a pattern, it'll really strengthen the case."

"Nice to know I'm not the only one," I say. "Do you want me to call my brother, or would you rather talk to him directly?"

I try to remain professional when I feel like dancing around the room. My dad did *not* have an affair with this creep's mother. I'm *not* losing my business. She's a fraud and I hope she ends up in jail.

"I'll contact him," he says. "I want to be sure all the legal pieces are solid if this ever goes to trial."

We return to my place in the late afternoon. I invite him to stay for wine and a snack, but he has an evening appointment.

"Next time, I promise," he says.

And there is a next time, just two weeks later. It is mid-November, and the weather is still holding.

"I've got more info," he says over the phone, "and I'd sure enjoy sharing it over another hike."

We opt for an easy walk to Mirror Lake. At lunch, he fills me in.

"I'm pretty sure you're not Evelyn's only 'sister.' I'm still digging, but she's used more than one name and lived in a bunch of places. I think she may have a partner, but I'm not sure. And I still can't figure out how she's getting those DNA results. As for the photo of her mom and your dad? It's clearly old, maybe blurry. She could've found a generic image, or maybe it's her actual parents. She tells you that's your dad, and you just... believe her?"

Back at the house, he agrees to a single glass of wine before heading home.

"One glass won't impair my driving," he says, "but two could cost me my license—and my career."

As he gets ready to leave, he takes my hands and looks at me.

"This has been such a great day," he says... and then he kisses me.

Just as suddenly, he pulls away.

"I'm sorry," he says. "I shouldn't have done that. I try to stay professional with clients. Please forgive me."

And then—he is gone.

Forgive him? No. Come back! Let's try a replay with a different ending. I realize I am really falling for this man.

For the next several days, a song loops in my head. When I was about five, my parents took Tommy and me to visit my mother's sister Anita. Anita's husband, Johnny, owned a bar in a small town. It felt like a grand adventure to sit on a barstool before the place opened. Johnny let me sip Coke and slipped me another when no one was looking. He was my hero.

The jukebox fascinated me, and Johnny gave me quarters to play whatever I wanted. I kept choosing one song—over and over:

"Oh, Johnny, oh Johnny, how you can love."

I don't remember the rest of the lyrics, but I remember the tune. It has become my favorite kind of earworm.

And now?

Now I really want to see Jonathan—dare I call him Johnny—again. Soon.

CHAPTER 37

JOHNNY, OH JOHNNY

It snows a bit at the end of November—a nice surprise. Not enough to ski on, but enough to spark hope. Then, in early December, it snows again—this time almost a foot. I call Jon (yes, we're now on shortened-name terms) and ask if he's serious about wanting to try cross-country skiing.

"Absolutely! I've only been once, but I really liked it. I don't have any gear, though. Can I rent some at Badger Pass?"

"Usually, but the resort isn't open yet. Early snow often melts quickly. But if you can fit into my dad's size 11 boots, we can ski up to the old fire lookout."

Two days later, he's here—and the boots fit.

It's just a mile up the dirt road, now covered with enough snow to hide stray rocks and branches. Jon's a bit awkward at first, so I show him the basic technique, and we slowly make our way uphill. At the top, we take off our skis and climb the steps to the lookout tower to admire the view.

"Why was this 'shack on stilts' put here?" he asks.

"In the 'olden days'—before satellite imagery—fire lookouts were placed on high points throughout the Sierra Nevada. At that time, fire suppression was the dominant strategy. These days, fires are often allowed to burn unless they threaten communities. Forests used to burn naturally every few years, clearing out underbrush and weak trees, helping the stronger ones survive. A ranger would stay up here for weeks at a time. His only job was to scan the horizon for smoke and call it in if he spotted any. This one was easy to access by road. Some others could only be reached on horseback, with supplies packed in by mule."

"Sounds like a boring job," Jon says, "but maybe if you were a writer or an artist needing solitude, it'd be perfect."

We're ready to head back down, so I teach him the basics of the snowplow technique. He picks it up quickly, and we return to the house around 4:00.

"Too early for wine and appetizers?" he asks.

"Not at all," I say, smiling. "I'm looking forward to relaxing a bit. I'm a little out of shape myself."

I make SOCCA while he opens a bottle of Chardonnay. It's a Mediterranean dish popular in southern France, where it's sold by street vendors. I whisk together two cups of garbanzo flour, two cups of water, a quarter cup of olive oil, and a teaspoon of salt. I pour it into a well-oiled 12-inch skillet, broil it for about five minutes, and then bake it at 450°F for fifteen more. Hot from the pan, it doesn't need anything—though some people add butter or grated cheese. We don't.

We share a second glass of wine, and I notice Jon doesn't seem in a rush to leave this time. I offer to make a simple supper of RACLETTE, and he eagerly agrees. I melt white cheese on a metal plate near the fire, nuke a few red potatoes, and bring out French bread for spreading the cheese. I add gherkins and some onion, and quickly pickle them in vinegar and sugar.

It's simple. Cozy. We just enjoy the atmosphere, the firelight, the wine—and each other. His arm goes around me. He pulls me closer. And we're kissing—long, lingering kisses that deepen slowly, deliciously.

He murmurs, "That sheepskin rug looks perfect... we could make love by the fire."

It turns out the hardwood floor beneath the rug isn't quite as romantic as we imagine. We move to the bedroom.

It's our first time, and while I haven't had much experience—just that one-off with Jack—I've lived through enough of Lori's stories to know the many ways it can go wrong. Awkwardness. Disappointment. Timing. Lack of comfort. But none of that happens.

It's as close to perfect as lovemaking can be. Jon is tender, caring, deeply present... and clearly very needy. I'm happy to meet him there.

We fall asleep in each other's arms, only to wake around midnight and return to lovemaking. He isn't in a rush to leave, and I'm in heaven. By morning, we're discovering each other all over again.

Eventually, though, we're starving. I slip out of bed and make us breakfast while he showers.

I have a large avocado—miraculously at its perfect ripeness, that magical five-minute window between underripe and overripe. I halve it, remove the pit, scoop out a bit more flesh, and crack an egg into each half. Into a 350°F oven they go for fifteen minutes.

Meanwhile, I slice three corn tortillas into strips and fry them in canola oil. MIGAS—peasant food turned trendy. I top them with cheese and diced green chiles. Jon and I sit down to breakfast like an old married couple—until:

"Oh, shit! I've got to get back to Fresno. All your fault! I completely forgot—I've got a client coming at noon."

Neither of us wants the moment to end, but he promises to be back as soon as he can.

"I'm almost done tying up the loose ends. Hopefully, I'll have Evelyn tied up for good. I'll have a full report to you and your brother before the end of the month."

"Why don't you plan to come here for Christmas?" I ask. "Tommy and his family will be here, and we can celebrate winning the Battle of Evelyn."

"I'd love to. But I need to drive my sister up to Santa Rosa to see our mom. She—Mom, not my sister—is in poor health and in a rest home. No way I'm letting her spend Christmas alone. But I'll definitely be back just after New Year's—for more skiing and... well, you know... uh..."

How adorable that he can't quite say it. Can't put words to what we've discovered.

After he leaves, he stays in my head.

Oh Johnny, oh Johnny... What a lover. This relationship is going places—I can feel it. I'm as dreamy as a lovesick teenager. Worse.

I start remembering those old jump rope rhymes from elementary school:

First comes love,
     Then comes marriage,
     Then comes mama with the baby carriage.

How silly. And yet, I can't stop. Maybe every girl goes through this phase. But at forty-five years old?

Still, I can't stop dreaming... making plans... futuring.

CHAPTER 38

ALMOST CHRISTMAS

Three days before Christmas, and I'm as excited as I used to be when I was six. Julie has been with me for the past week, and we've kept ourselves busy decorating the house and wrapping gifts. Still no tree, though. We've left that particular tradition to Tommy, who's arriving this afternoon with his wife, Gioia, their daughter, Lucy, who is Julie's age, and their son, Jaden, now thirteen.

Two more feet of snow fell yesterday, and more is expected on Christmas Day. Badger Pass has finally opened, so we'll be able to go both downhill and cross-country skiing. Though the income would be nice, I haven't booked any guests into the B&B over the holidays. Family time is treasure time.

This will be Tommy's first time seeing the house since the total makeover, and I expect he'll be surprised—hopefully not shocked—by the changes. The old house held so many memories for both of us, but I've adjusted to the new, much-improved version.

Since we still have some time before the family arrives, Julie and I grab our Nordic skis and take a quick tour around the neighborhood. The roads have been plowed, but there's a light dusting of snow over them, and though technically we're not supposed to ski on the roads, it's the simplest way to reach a trailhead. Everyone does it—especially in our area, where we live on a circular drive with few homes and even less traffic.

Most Californians don't think of snow as part of their lives. California conjures images of sun and beaches. But the Sierras—blanketed in snow—is what sustains the whole state. The spring thaw brings water to the Central Valley for crops and delivers drinking water to both Los Angeles and San Francisco. Without the Sierras' snowpack, California would be a desert.

We do the short ski up to the old fire lookout. The view never fails to stun me. I long to share with her the new and unexpected joy of my relationship with Jon—but I hold back. For now, it's just a "one-night stand," though in my heart I believe it will grow into something more. Still, I'm not ready to share that part of my life with the family just yet.

Instead, we take in the view together, looking east toward the Sierra Crest, completely carpeted in white, Buena Vista Peak rising gracefully from the slopes.

"Mom, point out Horse Ridge and Ostrander Lake for me," Julie asks. "It's hard to tell with everything covered in snow."

"See Buena Vista? Trace slightly north and west from there and that's Horse Ridge. You really can't make out much because we're looking at the top of it, and Ostrander Lake is tucked behind another ridge, so it's out of sight."

"Can you get us a reservation at the Ostrander Ski Hut sometime? I really want to go back."

"Already done," I grin. "I booked it last September—for all six of us —two days after Christmas. It's my Christmas gift to Tommy and his family, and I can't wait to see the look on his face when they open it. Gioia, Lucy, and Jaden have never been there, and I'm hoping they're in good enough shape for the nine-mile uphill trek. It's your gift too, but I've got something else in reserve for you."

We ski back home and have just enough time to shower before Tommy and his crew arrive—earlier than expected—in a blizzard of hugs and kisses.

Julie pouts a little at the absence of visible presents.

"Look, Little Jewel," Tommy says, using her nickname, "we weren't going to ship a trunk full of gifts, but I think you'll like the alternative."

He pulls a small, slightly crumpled but beautifully wrapped package from his suitcase and hands it to us. It's addressed to both of us, and he insists we open it right away.

"Tommy! Gioia!" I gasp. "Tickets to the Bracebridge Dinner at the Ahwahnee Hotel? Tomorrow night? Christmas Eve?" I'm stunned. "I can't think of a better gift. Well... maybe when you see my gift to all of you, it'll be a close contest."

Ignoring their playful begging for clues, I show them to their rooms to freshen up and then take them on the grand tour of the house. They're amazed by the changes—how the house now opens up to capture the beauty of the creek and sunsets.

"You turkey," Tommy laughs, falling back on his childhood nickname for me. "You told me you kept the windows for sentimental reasons! You wrote that we'd bring back old memories by cleaning them together again. You sneak!"

Our kids—and Gioia—look baffled as we both burst out laughing. We try, at the same time, to explain the epic frustration those windows caused when we were kids, our memories tumbling over each other.

We settle in with some wine, a hearty vegetable soup, French bread, and a CHOCOLATE/BANANA BREAD PUDDING for dessert. Then it's time to pop popcorn—some to eat, more to string into garlands.

The next day will bring the traditional Christmas Eve ritual, one we've preserved since our own childhoods. The menfolk—Tommy and Jaden—will set off to find the perfect Christmas tree. Technically, Julie and I already scouted the ideal one last year, but we'll still join the search and pretend to help "discover" this year's treasure.

It'll take all of us to haul a big tree uphill through the snow, but the result—watching it take over the living room in all its glory—will be worth it. We agree we'll all go together. The ladies will judge by height and symmetry. The gentlemen, by trunk size and ease of transport.

We'll spend the afternoon setting it up and decorating it with lights and memories. Then, we'll close out the perfect day by dressing up for the pageantry and magic of the Bracebridge Dinner at the Ahwahnee Hotel.

Can life get any better?

CHAPTER 39

THE BRACEBRIDGE DINNER

The tree is perfect. The twelve-footer Julie and I picked out last year is unanimously approved by the group, though it seems either to have grown over the year or, more likely, our estimate of its height was a little off. Either way, it clearly reaches closer to fourteen feet, and with the star on top, it nearly touches the 18-foot ceiling.

We need a ladder to decorate the upper branches, and I start to worry we might run out of ornaments before the whole tree is properly dressed. Fortunately, we have plenty of our popcorn garland and an abundance of lights, which help everything look beautifully festive.

After a well-earned rest in the afternoon, we dress in our best and head down the hill to the Ahwahnee Hotel for a truly memorable dinner.

The Bracebridge Dinner was established the same year the hotel opened—1927—but it took its current shape when Ansel Adams was asked to direct it in 1929. The idea for the dinner came from a Washington Irving story about a grand holiday feast at Bracebridge Hall in England. So, here we are—celebrating a fictional English Christmas dinner imagined by an American writer and brought to life by Ansel Adams in the heart of Yosemite.

The magnificent dining hall is completely transformed for the occasion. (Actually, occasions—the popularity of the event means several dinners are scheduled throughout the season.) The hall is decked out in holiday boughs and ribbons, and the raised alcove becomes a stage for the performers. In the center sit the squire and his lady—usually prominent locals from the Yosemite community—and to their left, the Parson, the lead speaker. All are dressed in period costume, and the effect is magical.

The menu is lavish and each course is introduced with a flourish as the chorus carries giant, elaborately crafted platters of "food" down the central aisle. These are made of papier-mâché—thankfully—since the real meal, served by the regular wait staff, is much more appetizing and entirely edible.

Throughout the evening, the chorus performs with festive flair, and the tall windows remain uncovered, allowing a view of "hungry villagers" peering in from the outside. It could be unnerving, but we know the truth: These are locals who have been invited to take part in the tradition and will be rewarded with a hearty meal after the show.

Tommy and I share the story of how, years ago, our parents played the squire and lady, and we, as kids, had been cast as those shivering, wide-eyed villagers. That role didn't require any acting skills—we really had been freezing out there, longing to be inside.

The dinner itself is as close to perfect as one could hope for, given the scale of the event and the pageantry surrounding it. The food, the atmosphere, the music, the shared memories—it all comes together seamlessly. Tommy and I take turns recounting our past experience with the Bracebridge, and as we look around the table, it is clear everyone is deeply grateful for the present moment, for each other, and for the beauty of Yosemite wrapped in snow and light.

CHAPTER 40

CHRISTMAS CRACKS

I wake up Christmas morning just after sunrise, which for me on this special day is really sleeping in. When we were kids, Tommy and I would try to see how late we could stay up on Christmas Eve and how early we could get up in the morning, buzzing with anticipation for what Santa had brought. Old habits die hard, and as I start making a pot of coffee, Tommy appears in the kitchen.

"Where are the kids?" we ask each other. Too old and sophisticated, apparently, to try and catch Santa in the act. Not us, though. Old habits, indeed.

I pull our traditional breakfast dish from the fridge, which I prepped the night before after we got back from the Bracebridge. This is STRATA, a dish our mom made every Christmas, and though it involves ingredients I'd normally never keep in my kitchen—white bread and processed cheese—it is tradition.

The night before, I sprayed a 9x12 Pyrex with Pam and made six simple sandwiches: a slice of processed cheese and a slice of ham (lunch-meat style), nothing else on the bread but a whisper of Dijon mustard and a touch of mayo. I'd beaten six eggs with three cups of milk and poured it over the sandwiches to sit overnight.

Once everyone is up and ready for presents, I slide it into a cold oven, turn it to 350°F, and let it bake for an hour while we open gifts.

Cups of coffee and cocoa rest on windowsills—no table space remains in the annual sprawl of presents, wrapping paper, and delighted squeals over gifts we never would have chosen for ourselves but will, somehow, become new essentials.

The kids aren't too old for the joy of it, after all. And honestly, neither are we.

My gift from Tommy, though, is a real puzzle—a beautiful gold bracelet with a cryptic note.

"What?" I ask, confused. "What does this mean?"

"What? What does the note say, dear sister?" he asks, all innocence.

"All will be revealed after dinner," I read aloud.

"So, I guess you'll just have to wait," he says with that maddening grin. Tommy has always enjoyed teasing me, but this is too much. He is being the Sphinx.

It snows lightly all morning. Picture-perfect Christmas weather. After lounging around in post-breakfast stupor, we decide a bit of skiing might help. Tommy's family hasn't skied since last year and needs to get their legs under them before our upcoming trip to Ostrander.

We strap on our cross-country gear and explore the neighborhood. I lead them down the hill behind the house—steep in parts and an excellent wake-up call for unused muscles. The hill flattens onto an old lumber road before narrowing and thickening with trees. Rather than push on, I take them right, along the road to a lookout point I've dubbed Couch Potato Point, in honor of an old couch that mysteriously appeared one year—and just as mysteriously disappeared a few years later. No one knows who hauled it up or hauled it away. A true neighborhood mystery.

The view is breathtaking. While Yosemite Valley is obscured to the right, we can see Highway 140 winding up through the Merced River Canyon from El Portal. To the north, the open stretch above the small community of Foresta unfolds, and beyond that, ridge after ridge ascends into the Sierra backcountry.

We earn our downhill and the uphill return, settling in for naps once we get back.

Dinner is our traditional prime rib with Yorkshire pudding and every side imaginable. Yorkshire pudding is essentially a savory "Dutch Baby"—one cup flour, one cup milk, and four eggs, whisked and poured into the beef fat left in the roasting pan after removing the meat. It bakes for thirty minutes while the roast rests, puffing up gloriously with golden crisp edges. Whether family or guests, everyone always finds delight in its irregular beauty.

We linger over cabernet after dinner, letting our meal settle before sampling the dessert Julie has made. But I can't wait any longer.

"Okay, big brother. Out with the surprise!"

"Settle in," he says, too casually. "It's a bit of a story."

"Dammit, Tommy. Stop teasing."

Realizing he might lose his audience, he begins.

"Since bad weather was forecast for DC on Christmas Eve—and flights were at risk—we changed our flight to the afternoon before. We managed to snag a couple of motel rooms in Fresno since we weren't arriving until after ten. It was too late to drive up here. In the morning, Gioia and the kids were barely awake and in no mood to head out right away, so I decided to see if Jonathan Steele was around."

My heart skips.

"He told me he had time for a quick visit since he was heading out of town for the holidays. Said he'd have a full written report ready for us after the New Year. But he gave me the highlights."

Jaden, thirteen-going-on-twenty, jumps in. "Dad always knows what to do. That detective knows he's gotta get it right for my dad. Don't f—"

"Jaden!" Tommy barks, soft but sharp. "Vocabulary. Go find a quiet space and consider more thoughtful phrasing."

I smile, even as my stomach clenches. Jaden isn't wrong—Tommy is formidable. I can only imagine him in court.

Tommy goes on. "Evelyn isn't her real name—no shock there. But since he wasn't sure of her true identity, he kept calling her Evelyn. He tracked down two other people she'd scammed, and their stories were almost identical. He believes she does have a half-sister and a boyfriend who works in a DNA lab. The working theory is simple: The boyfriend swapped names on the test results. Your name replaced the real half-sister's."

"I did one of those tests last winter," I say slowly, my mind racing.

"Exactly. It's actually a pretty simple con. She targeted you, made it personal, played it well. Steele is giving the report to the police—they're going to investigate."

"That simple?" I say, stunned.

"Yeah. And he was... impressive. Totally professional. His wife came by to pick him up for their trip to Sonoma. Pretty lady. Reminded me a bit of you."

My wine glass hits the floor, shattering. Red wine soaks into the white sheepskin rug like blood.

Julie and Lucy rush to clean it before anyone gets cut. Gioia glances at me, alarmed.

"Are you okay? You look like you might pass out."

"I'm fine. Really. I was just—surprised by how simple the scam was. Got caught up in it and wasn't paying attention to my hands. Wine abuse, for sure. It's been a long day. I think I'll turn in—we've got a big ski day tomorrow."

Of course, I don't say a word about my relationship with Jonathan. Not Jon anymore, not in my mind. That name now feels like a lie, too.

I brood in the bedroom. Furious. Not just at him—but at myself. I played along. I should've seen clues. Lori even asked: "How do you know he's not married?"

"I'd know," I told her. "I'm playing it cool." But that hadn't been true. I was swept up—first real romance since my divorce. I wanted it to be real.

"C'mon, Lori," I'd said. "You love the variety. I know this is different. I mean, how can you not trust a man named Jonathan Steele?"

"Or Steal," she'd quipped. "Maybe his *nom de plume* for assignations."

But I threw caution to the wind. Now, I sit on the edge of my bed, verbally thrashing myself. Not helpful. Not productive. And not conducive to sleep.

Brushing my teeth to the rhythm of creative swearing, I force myself to stop. I need to sleep or I'll never survive the long ski to Ostrander. And I'm not about to explain why.

I grab a mystery novel and let someone else's crime story carry me away—far, far from mine. Eventually, I float into sleep.

CHAPTER 41

OSTRANDER SKI HUT

We have great conditions for our ski into Ostrander Lake today. I've reserved two nights at the hut so we can have a layover day. All of us have our own Nordic (cross-country) skis, which have come a long way over the years. Ours have metal edges that make downhill maneuvering possible, and the bottoms are grooved for better grip. Back in the day, skis had slick bottoms, and you had to wax them for climbing or adjust for specific snow conditions—which, in California, change by the hour. To get up steeper hills, we would strap on seal skins, which were outrageously expensive. The hairs on the skins faced uphill so that if you started to slip, the loose ends would grab the snow and prevent you from sliding backwards. Thankfully, chemistry has intervened, and synthetic skins are now both affordable and effective.

As miserable as I was the night before, I don't have the luxury of dwelling on it. Breakfast has to be made—or at least supervised by me, the designated expert. Packs and equipment need to be prepped and organized. I'm determined to be on the trail by 10:00. We don't quite make that, but by 10:45, we're in the parking lot at Badger Pass and ready to start skiing just after 11:00.

"Am I dreaming?" Tommy says as he spots ski tracks already laid out along Glacier Point Road. "In the olden days, Gioia and my two dear children, the road had no tracks. It was true cross-country skiing, all the way. Oh, how we struggled, battling the elements—"

I join in the routine. "And we had to walk through snowdrifts to get to school, our toes and fingers suffering frostbite."

Julie cuts in, dryly, probably to make sure Lucy and Jaden aren't falling for it. "The road is tracked all the way to Glacier Point now. So, the first four miles are easy—unless snowshoers ignore the signs and trample the tracks, which they always do."

We decide to take the Bridalveil Trail on the way in—it's a gradual climb—then come out via Horizon Ridge, a long, gentle slope that allows for several parallel or telemark turns. Either route is a long ski, and in poor conditions or bad weather, it can take hours. But today, the snow is in pretty good shape. We climb slowly through the trees and reach Bridalveil Creek.

We have to cross the creek a few times, which can be tricky if snow levels are low. I always try to avoid returning that way—it's too easy to build speed on the descent and either miss a turn or hit a weak spot on the creek. Being wet and cold five miles from the ranger station at Badger Pass is not where you want to be. But uphill? Especially today? It's perfect. We press on.

I can't help thinking of a trip years ago when conditions seemed fine —until they weren't. I'd been leading a group of nine skiers to the hut. When we reached the mid-section of Bridalveil Creek, the trail markers were gone. Normally, not a problem—we were in a shallow bowl, and I could see the ridge we needed to reach. But the usual route was under-mined by the now-flowing creek.

I'd explained that we'd need to detour, arcing across the slope rather than following the bottom of the bowl. I pointed to our destination, but the group didn't seem to follow. We started the arc, and someone with a compass panicked.

"We're going the wrong way! Our leader is lost!"

Trying to explain geometry to exhausted skiers is not a great strategy. I tried again, thinking they'd come around. I kept going.

They didn't.

I reached the ridge, looked back, and realized no one had followed—except one skier who told me she couldn't convince the others. In my defense, if you've ever cross-country skied you know you can't keep looking back without risking a fall. But I should've made sure. I should've checked.

Now I had a choice: continue on with my one companion—we were only about a mile and a half from the hut—or turn around. The route ahead was mostly manageable. Just "Heart Attack Hill," which wasn't nearly as bad as its name suggested. A storm was rolling in and would probably hit in 30 to 45 minutes. We could've made it.

But the others had turned back. They could fall into the creek. They could get caught in the storm. They were already struggling with winter trail navigation. I couldn't risk it. I turned around, and we caught up with them. We herded them back, slow but steady, and by 7:00 that night, we were warm and safe in my house.

This trip, though, goes smoothly. We're all experienced and able to anticipate challenges—and there are few. The hut welcomes us. Other skiers are already there, and while each group brings their own food, there is plenty of friendly jostling for space on the Coleman stove and the wood-burning one. People share meals and stories. It's all very communal.

The next day, we explore the area. We practice our telemarks in Chili Bowl, then head east to a spot where we can climb the cliff face. It's still treacherous—ski a short distance, kick-turn on the vertical face, repeat. Not for the faint of heart. Afterward, we make our way to Buena Vista Peak. The views in every direction are stunning. Tommy and I point out peaks, naming each one, marveling at how much we remember. And how impressive we feel doing so.

We return home invigorated after three days of skiing. But soon after, Tommy, Gioia, and the kids fly back to DC.

I've played the perfect hostess. The wonderful sister. And they have no idea I want to scream about that lying, cheating, son of a bitch, Jonathan.

January arrives, and I realize just how quiet things are going to be. As I should have expected, business is slow—painfully so. The B&B has some weekend bookings and a reservation for the Martin Luther King holiday, but midweek is dead. February and March look the same.

Financially, it means my nine-month income has to stretch over twelve. Mentally, it means way too much time to stew.

I volunteer again to teach skiing to local school kids, which fills some hours, but not the chaos in my head. Not the Jonathan chaos. All I can do is wait for the final report. Not that I need one—I've already received all the clarity I need on that man.

It's Wednesday, around 4:00. I'm exhausted—teaching, tension, emotional whiplash. On the way home, I stop to check the mail.

There it is. A 9x12 envelope. Heavy. From Jonathan Steele.

I'm not surprised. I didn't expect a hand-delivery.

Or... maybe I had.

I build a fire. Pour a glass of wine. Settle in.

Then I open the envelope.

Surprise. It is the report. Very official. Detailed. Thorough.

No personal note. No apology. Nothing to suggest we've ever spent the night together. Nothing to acknowledge what had happened between us.

That bastard.

CHAPTER 42

FROM FROST TO FOAM

February comes, and I'm a prisoner of weather, slowly going stir-crazy. For reasons I can't quite explain, I'm getting very few lodging requests, aside from President's Day weekend. March doesn't look any better. Summer inquiries, of course, are pouring in.

Lori calls one Wednesday evening, and she's losing it too—but for entirely different reasons.

"Roach is simply unbearable," she says. "I'm not sure I can even make it to the end of the school year."

"You could come up here," I offer. "I don't seem to have any guests, and we could just hang out. I could teach you to ski."

"Except my car isn't built for snow—nor am I," she replies. "How about we plan a trip to the coast? The weather there in winter is almost always warm, and I'm tired of living in the constant cold and fog. When people talk about sunny California, they've clearly never spent winter in the San Joaquin Valley."

We agree to meet Friday in Fresno. I'll leave my car, and Lori will drive us to Cayucos, a small town on the central coast near San Luis Obispo.

"I'll take a 'well day' on Monday," she says. "Maybe even Tuesday. We can have a few days of blissful sunshine."

I ask Lori a couple of times about her paintings, and she suggests I come a bit early the night before we leave so she can give me a "tour." I've seen a few of her pieces before, usually just one at a time. She doesn't do much to promote herself, and I wonder how that might change if she really does quit teaching.

When I arrive around 4:30, she's already home from school and deep in her studio—which is actually just the second bedroom of her house. She greets me wearing a paint-smeared smock, a brush clamped between her teeth as she opens the door.

"Good timing!" she says, moving the brush to her hand. "I'm just adding the final touches to the first painting in a series of aspens from our trip. I'm more inspired than I've been in ages! I think the prospect of escaping Roach has finally unclogged my creative flow. Let's get a glass of Chardonnay, and I'll show you around."

She has several paintings hanging in the living room in various styles. I'm not sure if they're all hers, but she assures me they are. Three of them feature Yosemite. They're recognizable enough that I can place the locations, but they're not photographically accurate. Interpretive, I suppose, though I'm not sure of the right term.

"They remind me of jazz interpretations of old standards," I say. "Does that sound right?"

"I like that! I'm not a particularly good photographer. I don't have the patience for waiting around in perfect light or freezing for a dramatic fog shift. I never paint outside. No mosquitoes, no sunburn, no sudden storms for me—I like my air conditioned. And sometimes, it takes me forever to even decide what to paint."

"Well, you clearly know how to paint."

"But how I choose to interpret an idea is always changing," she says. "As you can see, my paintings vary in style. A lot of artists find their voice early, but maybe I'm just a slow learner. I feel like each painting needs its own voice—and honestly, sometimes when I see artists who stick to one style forever, I think, 'Maybe they're just bored.' Or lazy."

She chuckles. "I once went to a studio in Carmel, and the artist came up to me demanding I gush over his work. I told him he looked bored with it himself. He laughed and said, 'Will you marry me? You're the first honest person to walk in here!' I had to decline, but we had a great conversation about growth. I guess I can't help being a teacher."

She goes on. "That same trip, I saw a gallery featuring an artist who had been one of my students—or at least occupied space in my class-room. His name was Robert. First day of Commercial Art class, he announced, 'I'll be using this time to improve my painting skills instead of doing assignments.'"

"'Whoa,' I'd said at the time. 'You'll be doing the same assignments as everyone else. You might find there's a lot to learn on the commercial side, and that it'll help you sell your work.'

"He sniffed and said, 'She'll be in to see you.'

"By *she*, I assumed he meant his mother. Word was, she was a force. But thankfully, she never showed up. Robert eventually did the assign-ments—and was quite good. He even asked me to see some of his private paintings. I'd heard he was studying under an artist in Carmel, so I was expecting some skill. He had more than a bit. Especially for sixteen.

"We talked about his pieces—realistic landscapes. I suggested he observe tall grasses more carefully—his were a blinding emerald green, lacking natural variation. I doubted he listened, but at least we'd made peace. And I avoided a mom encounter.

"Years later, in Carmel, I see a painting by his teacher and suddenly understand Robert's green problem. Same green. But hey, the guy's successful, so who am I to judge? Then I spot a gallery with Robert's name. Same green grasses. I step in, hoping to say hello. An older woman greets me.

"'Is Robert here?' I asked. 'I taught him at Winston High.'

"'He's not here,' she snapped. 'And even if he is—you were never his teacher. You must be thinking of a painting he did of the school.'

"'Oh, you must be his dear mother!' I said. 'Tell him hello from me. And for the record, I don't usually confuse people with buildings. But I agree—I probably never taught him anything. Still using that dreadful green, I see!'

"I left, crossed the street, and stepped into another gallery. Two young men run it and filled me in.

"'His mother's ruining his life,' one said. 'He's actually a really nice guy—if you can get him away from her. She drives potential buyers out. Ask one critical question and she kicks you out.'

"The next time I visit, Robert's gallery is gone."

Back in Lori's living room, I ask, "So where do your ideas come from? Your styles and colors are all over the map."

"Good question," she says. "Where do your ideas come from when you cook? You never use recipes and everything tastes amazing. I guess I use my eyes like you use your nose and taste buds."

She walks me over to a painting. "This one's called *Victor*. A young Black student joined my class one year—cool, confident, didn't hold back like most new kids. Then one morning, I happened to be walking behind him in the hallway when someone shouted, 'Boy!' I don't know if it was directed at him, but he clearly thought it was. I watched his spine straighten, vertebra by vertebra. The fear was right there, just under the surface. I asked him later if he'd pose for me after school. This painting shows how he fits into the White world—and what lies underneath. A Black doctor once saw it at a party and said, 'You get it.' That was the best compliment I've ever gotten."

We move through her landscapes. "This one of El Cap reflected in the river? I was inspired by a German artist I saw at a museum. The curator's blurb about it was so pretentious I almost tore it off the wall. There's real art language—and then there's *art speak*, meant to confuse people into spending money they don't understand."

She shows me another. "The wilted iris? Part of a series. It started with tulips that were wilting in a vase. I realized how beautiful they were in decay, like women. We spend so much energy preserving youth. When beauty fades, so does perceived value. I asked my mother's friends all sorts of questions—made a series with paintings and poems about aging."

She continues, "*Taft Point*—I painted it to show the danger, the height, the granite. I didn't include the valley below. I wanted to evoke the fear, the scale, not document it. That's where painters have an advantage over cameras."

Then, "The Aspen painting? From our Sierra trip. Still not sure it's done. I keep returning to it. On the East Side of the range, the rise is so abrupt—so gray, no lush lead-in. Then the aspens turn gold, and the contrast is breathtaking. I wanted the painting to shake, like they do in the wind."

Friday morning, the drive from Fresno to Cayucos takes just three easy hours. We've booked the Seabreeze Inn, right by the beach. Cayucos is charming—one main street, a few restaurants, and a five-mile beach stretching to Morro Bay. At low tide, it makes for an incredible walk. High tide makes return tricky; ten miles in sand is no joke.

Unlike the glamour of SoCal or the polish of Carmel and Monterey, the Central Coast is still a bit under the radar. Quieter. Colder water. Beginner surf. But less traffic, great beaches, and fabulous wine country. It suits us.

That night at the Sea Shanty over fish dinners, Lori drops her news. "I love it here. I'm moving. I'm quitting in June. I want a studio and a fresh start. And I think you should come too."

"Don't be silly," I say. "I've got a business to run."

"Not much in winter, it looks like. I have a plan—hear me out. We pool resources. Buy a duplex or something with a separate apartment. I'll live in the smaller space and make it my studio. You stay in the larger unit during winter and rent it out for the rest of the year. I'll oversee guests. You can run your Yosemite business online."

I'm not sure I'm ready to give up skiing or solitude every other day. Then again, I'm very ready to give up solitude. Over our second glass of wine, the idea starts sounding better and better.

The next morning, we take a long walk on the beach and have smoked fish tacos for an early lunch. We wander around town—small enough to cover easily—and peek into real estate windows.

"Obviously, this won't be cheap," we say, nearly in unison.

But I'm warming to the idea.

Later, Lori says, "Let's check out the local bar tonight. See if there's any action."

"You mean... pick up guys?"

"Sure! I'll teach you how!"

"I'm not sure I want that on my résumé—but I could probably use a few pointers from the master."

Cayucos' nightlife is... limited. Two bars, both walkable. Nice for drinking, not for options. We peek into both.

"Let's try Morro Bay," she says. "Just one drink—or two. And maybe live music."

We find a place, but as soon as we walk in, it's clear: We're the oldest women there, the music is loud, and the dancing isn't really dancing. More like a prelude-to-nakedness swaying.

Lori stays hopeful. "Come on. One drink."

Our beers have barely arrived when two guys come over and ask us to dance. Mine leans in during a quieter song.

"My name's Johnny. I come here a lot, but haven't seen you before."

"First time."

"I really like older women. More experienced, if you know what I mean..."

Should I walk off the floor now?

He leans in again. "This place is kind of boring. My friend's got a great apartment nearby. Fully stocked bar. Killer sound system."

Back to my seat.

Lori's already there. "What'd yours say?" I ask.

"After telling me he liked older women, he said: 'This place is kind of boring. I have an apartment nearby...'"

"You've got to admire the coordination."

They're not wrong. The place is boring. And we know just where to go—back to the motel, with some decent wine and soft music. Alone.

CHAPTER 43

A PRODUCTIVE EVENING

"So," Lori says over breakfast, "have you thought more about my idea?"

"Yeah, I have. And since we now officially have nothing better to do —no handsome dudes in our lives or our beds—let's talk some more."

"Well," she says, eyes bright, "assuming we can find a property we like, I really think we could go into business together. But I want to do it legally—not just two friends winging it. We need to know exactly how much each person is investing and how we'll divide any profits."

"When my parents died," I say, "the trust stated that I'd get the house and Tommy would get the cash equivalent. Then we split the rest of the estate evenly. I used my share to help finance my current place-slash-business. I still have a small mortgage, but I cover it with my profits. I put the money from selling the Winston house into investments, but I could cash those in. Your place should sell for about the same, and that could give us a solid down payment."

"See, Moni! I knew I had a great idea. But tell me more about how your business actually runs. I'm sure there are some unexpected headaches we'd need to be ready for."

I barely start to explain when she cuts in.

"That's an awful lot of work to be doing by yourself. Do you ever hire help?"

"I usually handle it. Even if I have to drive to Oakhurst for groceries, I manage. But if I have to unexpectedly run to Fresno—that's a four-hour round trip—I try to get someone to cover. I haven't had much luck."

"Why not?"

"Well," I sigh, "Yosemite West has a small pool of people who want part-time work... or maybe a small pool of people who want to work at all. One couple quits halfway through their first day. I explain the chores before leaving for Fresno at ten. I come back around 3:30 to find that two of the three rooms haven't even been touched. I panic—scramble to clean everything myself. When I call them to ask what happened, they say, 'We went home for lunch and decided it was too much work. We're independent contractors, so we set our own schedule.'"

I shake my head. "They were certainly independent. Click."

Lori laughs, shaking her head.

"Another couple drove up from Wawona. They seemed okay, so I used them twice. The next day, I ran into a neighbor who asked why the sheriff and a park ranger had been to my house. What? Turns out, the couple got into a fight while cleaning. She called 911. The park ranger arrived first, then the sheriff, who arrested the guy and took him to jail in Mariposa. He was released the next day and apparently had to take a cab back to Wawona. Must've cost a fortune. The woman was still fuming when I talked to her. Said she was moving away. Fine by me."

I sip my coffee and continue, "Then I tried hiring a single woman from the area. I came home to find her slowly dusting my bookshelves—more browsing than dusting. The rooms were only half-cleaned, laundry undone. I dread Fresno days."

"I'm sure we'll have a bigger pool of workers here on the coast," Lori says, "but I'm not convinced the attitude would be any better. If we do a vacation rental instead of a B&B, it would eliminate a lot of issues, but we'd still have to figure out how to run it. I really don't want to be hands-on. I'm coming here to paint. So, I say we charge enough to pay for a full-service package: check-ins, cleaning, repairs."

"I'm totally with you. There's no way I'm doing another B&B. My business is interesting, but I don't need more."

"But where would we live?" she asks.

"Maybe we could find a duplex. Two bedrooms each. Or something with a separate cottage."

"I don't need much space," she says. "Just a bed and a studio. I'm not planning on getting social here, whatever social life here even looks like. And you wouldn't be around full-time anyway, mostly just winters and maybe a few other times. Your half could be the rental."

She pauses, then adds, "Let's look around more tomorrow, get a feel for the different areas."

Sunday, we drive through several of the smaller towns nearby, checking out real estate windows but not contacting any agents yet. There are lots of listings. A lot to think about.

That evening, we sit at the motel sorting through the fliers we've picked up.

"I'm not saying it's a bad idea," I tell her, "but I'm kind of shell-shocked at the prices."

"Me too," she admits. "But we'd be putting two incomes together—that should help. I just want to make sure you really like the idea."

"Well, let's say I'm warming to it. I definitely think, if we do this, we need to be near the beach. Like, walking distance."

"Absolutely. Any towns stand out to you?"

"Well, San Luis Obispo is too far inland. Pismo Beach is too commercial. I really liked Avila Beach. It's at the end of the road, which gives it a quiet, tucked-away feel. The beach is nice, and I've heard it's often sunny when the other towns are covered in fog."

"I agree," she says. "Morro Bay feels a bit too big, but it does have a lot going for it—Morro Rock, hiking, sailing, golf. Still, I lean toward Cayucos. Maybe something between Morro Bay and Cayucos could work."

"I'm taking a 'well day' tomorrow," she adds with a grin, "so we can focus on house shopping. Let's contact a couple of agents and see if this is even feasible. No rush—I can't do much until I quit in June and sell my house—but I want to get a sense of what's possible."

CHAPTER 44

HOW TO NOT GET ARRESTED IN YOSEMITE

Back home, I find myself with plenty of time to think about this possible new venture. Eventually, I pick up the phone and call Tommy to get his thoughts.

"Moni," he says, "I think it sounds like a really sharp idea. You could run the B&B for seven months and then take most of the next five off—to be at the coast, ski, travel, whatever you want. Obviously, you and Lori need to do everything totally legally. If the law firm that helped with the estate doesn't do real estate, I'm sure they can recommend someone."

He pauses, then adds, "I didn't want to say anything at Christmas, but you sure looked tired."

I'm not about to tell him the real reason for that "tiredness," but he's not wrong. The business has become all-consuming. It's already too much. I'm finally understanding the infamous three-year burnout.

"Tommy, I really appreciate your insight and support. I'll be checking in with you a lot to make sure I'm not making a huge mistake."

"And don't hesitate to ask me for financial help if you need it. I think this could be a good investment. I could be a silent partner. A little more money might let you consider a more upscale property, which should bring in a better return—so don't feel like you're stuck on the lower end!"

"Wow. I like that. I'll run it by Lori. I'm sure she'll prefer 'upscale' to 'down!'"

Predictably, she loves the idea of more money to play with. We decide to plan two more scouting trips to the coast before April rolls in and my business locks me into Yosemite. I laugh at the irony of that thought. Locked into Yosemite? Not exactly a prison sentence.

Since we've narrowed down our location and hired a real estate agent, things are a lot easier. But once April comes, I'll have to trust Lori to continue the search and maybe even make a decision. I won't be able to get away on weekends, and she can't leave school during the week.

In the meantime, I know I need to use my slower months wisely—to analyze the business and make improvements. One glaring time-waster becomes immediately obvious: the number of hours I spend explaining Yosemite to guests. Over and over, the same questions, the same answers. I need a solution that doesn't make me want to throw myself into the Merced River.

So I decide to make a brochure. Something simple, chatty, not formal—just the essentials that can go in each guest room and also be posted on the website. Here's what I draft:

WHILE YOU'RE HERE...

Information for Your Visit to Yosemite

THE BASICS

Yosemite National Park is actually larger than the state of Rhode Island, but unless you're staying for several days, you'll likely spend most of your time in Yosemite Valley. That's where you'll find the iconic rock formations—Half Dome and El Capitan—and the waterfalls: Bridalveil, Yosemite Falls, Vernal, and Nevada Falls.

The Valley itself is seven miles long and one mile wide, and with five million visitors annually, it can get very crowded, especially in summer. Once you've found a parking spot (no small feat), it's best to walk or use the free shuttle system.

Key areas in Yosemite Valley:

• *Yosemite Village* – Visitor Center, Museum, Ansel Adams Gallery, a grocery store, and a few eateries.

• *Curry Village and Yosemite Lodge* – Lodging and dining.

• *The Ahwahnee Hotel* – The most elegant (and expensive) place to dine, but well worth a visit even if you're not eating there.

Driving around the eastern part of the Valley, you'll notice many houses and dorms. These are for park rangers and concession staff. The housing isn't glamorous, but the views are unbeatable. It's very much like a self-contained small town. There's an elementary school, but high schoolers are bused to Mariposa an hour away. A medical clinic handles basic issues, but serious injuries are airlifted out by helicopter.

OUTSIDE THE VALLEY – DO NOT MISS

Two other areas inside the park are about a 30-minute drive from the Valley and absolutely worth visiting:

• *Glacier Point* – Offers a breathtaking view of the Valley floor and Yosemite's high country.

• *Mariposa Grove* – Near the South Entrance, this grove of giant redwoods is awe-inspiring.

You can drive to both or take a tour bus, which provides a narrated experience with helpful info.

If you have more time, plan day trips to two other regions of the park:

• *Tuolumne Meadows* – At 9,000 feet, this high alpine area is framed by peaks soaring above 12,000. The Tuolumne River winds through green meadows, and there are plenty of hiking trails. Or just wade (if you dare!) in the glacial waters.

• *Hetch Hetchy Valley* – A lesser-known twin of Yosemite Valley with towering granite cliffs and waterfalls. Sadly, the valley floor is now a reservoir—dammed (or, in my opinion, damned) by San Francisco for its water supply. To get there, you leave the park at the north entrance, then re-enter a few miles later. The drive through the canyon is beautiful, and in spring, the wildflowers are spectacular. While you can't swim or wade, the hiking is excellent once you cross the dam.

YOSEMITE SEASONS

• *Spring* is magical, especially May, with roaring waterfalls and wildflowers.

• *Summer* is beautiful but extremely crowded.

• *Fall* brings spectacular colors—dogwoods, maples, and golden oaks.

• *Winter* is pure snow-globe magic but also means chain restrictions and potential road closures.

If you're visiting in winter, you'll likely need rental tire chains, especially if it snows during your visit. Most people don't know how to install them, so for a fee, local "chain monkeys" will take care of it for you. (Trust me—it's worth every penny.)

Be aware: Highway 120 from Crane Flat to Lee Vining is closed in winter and often doesn't reopen until mid-June. I always ask about your route when you book so I can give a heads-up if something changes. Rockfalls, snow, and closures are surprisingly common.

YOSEMITE WEST

We're a small private community inside the Park, between Wawona and Yosemite Valley, at 6,000 feet. My bed and breakfast is tucked into a forest of pine, cedar, fir, oak, and dogwood, with spring wildflowers, fall color, and peaceful snowfall in winter.

We have no commercial services, so no restaurants or stores. If you arrive late, you might find everything closed in Wawona or the Valley. But not to worry, I keep frozen emergency meals on hand.

Our spot is peaceful, with a creek at the base of the hill, a picnic table, and a hammock for tired feet and sunset views. We also have local trails and old dirt roads for exploring when you need a break from the crowds.

TRAFFIC ISSUES

Let me be honest: traffic in Yosemite Valley is legendary—and not in a good way.

You'll likely face a wait at the entrance station (sometimes 30+ minutes), which you'll avoid by staying inside the Park with me. Still, once in the Valley, many guests come back grumbling:

"The traffic was awful!"

"We couldn't find parking anywhere."

"Why don't they fix this?"

The Park Service agrees. They've tried different solutions for decades, but the problem persists: too many cars, not enough space.

Some have asked why we don't use buses like Zion National Park. The answer? Yosemite has four entrance roads, and 70% of visitors enter by one route and leave through another. Not exactly bus-friendly. While we do have a system called YARTS, it's mostly used by employees. Tourists, understandably, prefer the flexibility of their own cars.

Many proposed solutions—giant parking lots, remote shuttle systems—run into issues: land destruction, high costs, seasonal limitations, and local opposition.

The eco-friendly shuttle within Yosemite Valley is free and runs frequently, but it's often packed. Most guests end up walking anyway.

HOW TO (ACCIDENTALLY) BREAK THE LAW

Yosemite is a federal park, so Park Rangers are federal law enforcement officers. That means if you get caught speeding, you're not just paying a fine—you're committing a federal offense.

We have two kinds of rangers:

• *Naturalists*–the ones who explain wildlife, geology, and trees.

• *"Gun rangers"*–the law enforcement officers who handle traffic violations, criminal behavior, and emergencies.

There's even a federal courthouse in Yosemite Valley. And yes, the judge is a federal magistrate. If you're from Vermont and think you can ignore that speeding ticket—think again. You might get arrested in your home state and flown back to face the judge. And not directly. You might go from Vermont to Chicago to Houston to Fresno—slowly.

So, I tell my guests: Don't get a ticket.

Here's my best advice:

If you're returning from a dinner at the Ahwahnee, roll down your window until you pass Yosemite Lodge. This prevents any alcohol odors from collecting in your car.

Come to a full stop at every stop sign—even if no one's around.

Obey the 25-mph speed limit between the Ahwahnee and the Lodge. Drive 24–26 mph. Go slower, they might suspect you're impaired. Go faster, and you're speeding.

Rangers do assume that Ahwahnee diners have enjoyed some wine. Let's not give them probable cause.

So far? I haven't lost a guest yet!

Another tip: Don't camp outside designated areas. People sometimes try to rough it in the meadows when campgrounds are full. That's another federal offense.

Park Rangers are passionate about preserving this place—for you, the wildlife, and future generations. They're not being fussy. They're just protecting the Park from people acting like idiots.

Writing the brochure feels strangely satisfying. Like I'm reclaiming time and sanity one paragraph at a time.

The bigger question still hangs in the air: Can I actually split my life between two beautiful places? Can I keep my roots in Yosemite and branch out to the coast?

Only time and a few more real estate fliers will tell.

CHAPTER 45

KNOCK, KNOCK

It's 6:30 in the evening, and the sky has already finished its display of deepening blues—something I enjoy from the deck despite the chill. Now I'm in my office near the entryway, catching up on some book-keeping. It's been an incredibly slow winter. Despite my best advertising efforts to promote the wonders of Yosemite in the off-season, it's turned out just like the year before: Deadsville.

I've hoped to draw more skiers, but few actually show. Badger Pass is a good family ski resort, but it's not exactly thrilling for advanced skiers. And since my B&B is clearly geared toward adults, not families, the bookings are minimal. Reservations are finally starting to pick up, but I've definitely learned my lesson about saving for a rainy day. In my case, it's been a whole snowy season of stretching the income just to make it through.

With Jonathan out of the picture, things feel dull—lonely, even. Sure, I enjoy teaching the kids to ski and getting in quite a bit of cross-country skiing myself. I even make a daily ski run down to the mailbox. But the truth is, I'm bored. More than a little.

And then comes a knock at the front door.

That alone is unusual. I'm not expecting any guests, and we're far enough off Wawona Road that there isn't exactly walk-in traffic. I open the door to find—of all people—Jack. As in Jackass, my ex-husband. I should've installed one of those peepholes years ago. Could've saved myself from this entire scene.

"Jack? What are you doing here?"

"Can I come in so we can talk? It's pretty cold out here."

"Sure," I say, though I'm still baffled. "I'll make us some hot cocoa, though I can't imagine what brings you up this way."

He deflects, glancing around. "Wow. You've really done a great job with this place. Last I saw it, it was pretty decrepit."

Okay, I'll admit—it's nice to get a compliment, even from an ex. I haven't really thought about it, but he hasn't seen the B&B since the divorce. So I give him a quick tour of the guest rooms before we head upstairs. While I stir the cocoa, he keeps complimenting my vision and hard work.

But I'm not in the mood for empty praise.

"Jack, I think you're laying it on a little thick. Why are you really here?"

"You always did like to cut straight to the point."

"And I'm asking again. It's a two-hour drive from Winston. You obviously planned this trip and hoped I'd be home. So what gives?"

He fidgets. Mumbles. Digs his toe into the rug. Finally, the truth comes out.

"Giselle and I broke up."

"So?" I ask, deadpan. "That still doesn't explain why you're here."

Of course, I already know they've broken up. Lori keeps me well informed of all the small-town gossip. Giselle sold her house and moved back to San Francisco months ago. Jack's cycled through the few single women in town and is now apparently branching out to Fresno.

"I miss you," he says suddenly. "I didn't realize what a good thing I had until you were gone. I've got a lot of regrets. I'm hoping... maybe we can start over."

Two years ago, that might have made me crumble. Might've made me question if I'd been too hasty in filing for divorce. But not anymore. This man feels like someone I used to know. I don't want him back. I can't even summon the sarcasm or bitterness I thought I'd feel. I just say, quietly, "I'm sorry that you have regrets, but I don't. I'm running a business. I'm happy with my life. I hope you can find peace, Jack, but our life together is over. It's going to stay over."

I stand up. "I'm really busy, and I need to get back to work. Please leave."

He looks stunned—like no woman has ever said no to him before. And maybe none has. But I'm calm. Direct. Unmoved. When he doesn't move fast enough, I gesture toward the stairs and follow him to the front door. I wait to make sure it latches behind him, then return to my office and my underwhelming income reports.

Still no word from Evelyn—which is both comforting and maddening. I have no idea if the police have arrested her, or if they're even interested. And if she had contacted me, what would I have done? Called Jonathan? Reported something to him? No, thanks.

Toward the end of February, I call Tommy, fishing for updates without revealing anything about my own involvement with Jonathan. I'm not about to tell my brother I've had an affair with the private investigator he's been paying. I already feel like a fool. No need to confirm it.

"Hi, Tommy. Just wondering if you've heard anything from Jonathan about Dear Evelyn?"

"No. I really don't expect to."

"Why not?"

"I thought he said he turned everything over to the police."

"Well, yeah. But what happens next?"

"Come on, Sis. Don't you ever read detective novels? The cops investigate. If there's a crime, they might arrest her—or her accomplice. But these things take time. It's probably not a top priority. If there's a murder or kidnapping in their jurisdiction, guess which case they'll focus on."

"But will we ever know what happens? Will Evelyn ever get her comeuppance?"

"Maybe. Maybe not. They might call us for a statement. Or maybe she's scammed someone local and we'll never be needed. Maybe the cops are setting her up with a little entrapment right now."

"Why don't you call Jonathan and check in?"

"Call him yourself. I've got work. You're the one in your slow season."

"Fine," I tell him. "If I don't hear anything, I'll give him a call."

Which I know is a lie. I have no intention of calling Jonathan. But now Tommy will assume I have, and I can always make up some vague statement if he ever asks what Jonathan said.

So, back to frustration—also known as Square One. (Though honestly, where does that phrase come from? And is there a Square Two? Square Three? Do we mark progress by geometrical metaphors?)

I sigh and turn back to my bookkeeping.

And then—another knock.

"Who's there?"

"It's Jack."

Unbelievable. Haven't I been crystal clear just minutes ago? I storm toward the door, my blood starting to boil.

I fling the door open and shout, "Can't you get it through your thick skull? We're through!"

Only... It's not my ex.

Standing on the porch, clearly startled and about to walk away, is the other Jack. My contractor. My one-night stand. Not Jackass—just Jack.

As he turns, I see his face under the porch light. He looks a bit caught off guard, and rightfully so.

Instinctively, I call out, "Jack! Wait!"

CHAPTER 46

THE BEGINNING (ALMOST)

The next morning, I wake up at 6:00 as I always do, ready to take a short run and start making breakfast. As one foot emerges from the sheets, I remember that there weren't any guests last night, just the two uninvited Jacks, both gone. I have the whole day to myself! I have my whole life to myself: mine to organize, mine to plan, mine to live the way I want to.

Wrapped in my fuzzy robe, I enjoy a cup of coffee on the deck, admiring the beauty surrounding me—the morning sky with the pines, firs, and oaks whispering in the light breeze, the sun reflecting off the morning dew.

What I've done these past three years is a major accomplishment. Renovating an old cabin and turning it into a thriving business wasn't easy, particularly with obstacles like Jack, Roach, and Evelyn. And I shouldn't forget dear Jonathan, that cheating creep!

But I did it! I survived. I am here. And I got here on my own.

I realize that women aren't always used to accomplishing things on their own. Even though attitudes have changed a lot over the past fifty years, there's still this lingering sense that men do and women cheer them on. But here I am, a successful businesswoman planning another venture. Maybe I'll hand out some pompoms to two Jacks and a Jonathan.

Rah rah, zip boom bah—Monica! Monica!

Big hurrah!

What comes next? No one can predict the future, but I can plan. I can hope. Will Lori and I be able to create a business on the coast? Maybe. We've got a good start.

Will I ever find a romantic partner? Possibly Jack, or someone I haven't met yet. But here's the thing—I don't need a romance to be a success. I've already proven that.

I have a life I love. A future that's mine to shape. And as the morning sun warms my face, I know this for certain:

Whatever comes next—I'm ready.

Chapter 47

Recipes from the Yosemite Peregrine Bed and Breakfast

My husband Don and I ran our bed and breakfast, *The Yosemite Peregrine*, for eighteen years—and we loved it! I did most of the cooking, and he was a natural entertainer. Breakfast was served at 8:00 each morning (though I made picnic breakfasts for guests heading out on early hikes). The table would be set in advance with colorful placemats, napkins, and fresh flowers. Don helped guests get their coffee or tea, providing conversation while I cooked. If anyone tried to get me to join in, I'd say, "You can have conversation or food—but not both from me —as I get confused and forget ingredients or burn something!"

For guests from foreign countries, I tried to use flavors they'd be familiar with, even if they didn't recognize the specific food.

Our six guests would gather around our beautiful redwood burl table after pouring their coffee. Don would regale them with Yosemite stories and trivia while I finished up breakfast. He'd been the U.S. Magistrate Judge in Yosemite for twenty years and had plenty of tales to tell—he was a natural!

After beverages were secured, I served a first course, usually fruit in some form. Breakfast parfaits, which could be made in advance, were a favorite. Yin-Yang soup had to be made at the last minute by Don and me, but it was always a crowd-pleaser. If the main course featured a lot of fruit, I served something small and savory first.

We tried to advise people about hiking options, though some ignored our suggestions and later wondered why their hike didn't go as planned. A frequent mistake was thinking they could climb Half Dome after a leisurely breakfast. We explained it was a ten-hour round trip with a 4,000-foot elevation gain—pretty grueling even if you're in great shape!

Once, we had a couple from England, so I made a "Dutch Baby"-style pancake (essentially Yorkshire pudding batter that puffs dramatically in the oven). For this version, I placed sautéed apple slices and sausage pieces in a wheel pattern in the bottom of the pan before adding the batter and baking. I announced it could be eaten savory, as is, or sweetened with syrup. The British woman jumped up and said, "I hate American breakfasts!"—then stalked off! (My brain was busy parsing "Yorkshire pudding" and "American breakfasts" and getting confused.) Her partner stayed calmly at the table, and I carried on as if nothing had happened. We didn't see her again for breakfast—or for wine hour—though her companion never missed either. We wondered if they took separate flights back to England.

Another time, a guest announced she might be having a miscarriage just as I was serving the main course! She'd been worried since 4:00 a.m. but "didn't want to disturb us." Though it was May, it was snowing heavily, and the nearest small town was over an hour away in good weather. Leaving our other guests momentarily abandoned, we helped the couple load their gear into their car. Don drove their vehicle—which had neither four-wheel drive nor tire chains—and had them follow him in our all-wheel drive Subaru. Luckily, he was able to flag down a snow-plow driver on Highway 41, who kindly cleared the road ahead of them. (She didn't have a miscarriage, fortunately—though when I learned her doctor had advised against high-altitude travel and she'd come anyway, I was a little less sympathetic.)

Most of the time, things went more smoothly!

Writing these recipes was almost harder than writing the novel because I seldom use recipes, and when I do, I tend to tinker. I have a good sense of the basics of cooking and baking, and I learned a lot from

Julia Child's *Mastering the Art of French Cooking*. I'd prep as much as possible during the day and freeze doughs to bake in the morning. Some main dishes could be made in advance and reheated in the microwave— which got a lot of use!

We rarely had guests with allergies. In eighteen years, we had no gluten-free requests. The most common "allergy" was eggs, and when questioned, most guests admitted they simply didn't like fried eggs because their mothers made them eat them. I became adept at disguising eggs, as you'll see in the "Peregrine Eggs" recipe. One of my favorite recipes was Breakfast Fajitas, which features scrambled eggs, but tofu could easily be substituted for egg-averse guests.

Enjoy some of our favorite recipes on the following pages.

BREAKFAST FAJITAS

Set up a "Lazy Susan" (who was that woman?) with the following: shredded cheese, sour cream, chopped green onions, chopped cilantro, salsa, and chorizo (I use soy chorizo). Scramble 1–2 eggs per person and divide between commercial corn taco shells (two each). Guests help themselves to Susan's goodies.

BREAKFAST EGG ROLLS:

This is a basic recipe with several applications. Beat 10 eggs and place in a lined 10x15-inch pan. I prefer non-stick foil, as you can mold the foil to fit the back of the pan perfectly, preventing sticking. Bake for 15 minutes at 350°F. Remove from oven and, as soon as you can, roll lengthwise. Then let it resume its flat shape. (Somehow, it seems to retain the memory of the roll, so when you fill it, it rolls back easily.)

1. Spinach: Make a spinach egg roll by adding frozen chopped spinach (drained) mixed with cream cheese. Spread on the flattened egg roll and roll up. Cut the roll into three pieces—you now have three five-inch rolls. Cut each piece on a diagonal, leaving one inch at the top and bottom. Stand vertically. I dubbed these "Half Dome Omelettes" and placed some sautéed mushrooms at the base. Serve with biscuits or savory scones. These are very pretty!

2. Mexican: Grated cheese and chopped green chilis. Re-roll and cut into one-inch slices. These are good savory starters.

BASIC BREADS

BISCUITS/SCONES:

You can find an amazing number of biscuit recipes, but I prefer this one—it's super simple and doesn't require cutting in butter or shortening. I often make bread doughs in the afternoon when less busy and then freeze them. You pull out what you need in the morning and bake following the original instructions for time and temperature; they usually take only a minute or two longer.

I also make square biscuits rather than round, as using the traditional shape requires cutting and re-rolling scraps, which is time-consuming. I use this same basic recipe for savory scones or add 2 tablespoons sugar and ½ teaspoon cinnamon for a sweet biscuit or scone.

- 2 cups flour
- 2 tsp baking powder
- ½ tsp salt
- 2 tsp sugar
- 1 ¼ cups heavy cream

Just mix and pat out about ¾ inch thick on a sheet of floured wax paper. Cut shapes and either freeze or bake (ungreased pan) at 450°F for about 15 minutes.

For savory scones, add a good handful of grated cheddar cheese to the flour mix and cut back a bit on sugar. For sweet scones, add an extra tablespoon of sugar and a teaspoon of cinnamon. You can add fruits such as raisins, chopped cranberries, etc. Be brave! You really don't need a recipe to make simple changes.

HONEYMOON BISCUITS:

Every marriage needs a bit of spice. Add a tablespoon of ground black pepper to your biscuit recipe.

DEDE'S OVERNIGHT COFFEE CAKE:

My favorite recipe from a friend. Mix most of this the night before and finish in the morning.

- 2¼ cups flour
- ⅔ cup each white and brown sugar
- 1 tsp cinnamon
- ¼ tsp cardamom
- ¾ cup oil

Mix and remove ¾ cup. Add 1 cup of chopped pecans or walnuts and 1 teaspoon of cinnamon to this mix. This will be the topping.

In the morning, add to the flour/sugar mix:

- ½ tsp salt
- 1 tsp baking powder
- 1 egg, beaten with 1 cup buttermilk

Pour batter into a greased 9x13 pan and spread topping over the top.

Bake at 350°F for 40–45 minutes.

You can put fruit such as chopped rhubarb or cranberries on the batter and then cover with the topping.

PLUM SURPRISE COFFEE CAKE:

Use any basic coffee cake recipe—I prefer one with cinnamon for this. You will need a bundt pan, sprayed with Pam. Cut 6 plums in half and remove the pits. Place an inch of batter in the bundt pan. Place a whole plum in each wide section (cut side vertical). Cover with the remaining batter. After baking and cooling for a while, remove cake from pan and slice through the plums. When you serve, you should have cake surrounding a plum half.

CREPES

In a blender, pour 1 cup of whole milk and 1 cup of water. Add 4 eggs, 2 cups of flour, ½ teaspoon of salt, and 2 tablespoons of melted butter.

Crepes are so much fun to make in quantity! You need to set up your cooking area correctly, as once you start, you'll be working at the speed of light! You will need three pans—two about 8 inches and a larger third pan. Place the two smaller pans on the front burners and the larger pan on the back burner. Set up an area on your counter to receive the crepes, covered with a large dishtowel (not terrycloth). Heat your pans on medium.

1. Pour enough batter to cover pan 1 and swirl quickly to cover.
2. Immediately pour batter into pan 2.
3. Turn the crepe from pan 1 into pan 3 and immediately refill pan 1 with batter.
4. Dump pan 3 onto the counter and put pan 2 into pan
5. Refill pan 2.
6. Keep going!

When you're totally exhausted or run out of batter, sit down and reward yourself with a glass of wine! The crepes will cool rapidly, and you can stack them in batches of 6–8 and freeze until needed. They can be filled with fruits or savory fillings.

DUTCH BABY (YORKSHIRE PUDDING):

One cup of flour, one cup of milk, and four eggs in the blender. (For Yorkshire pudding, the batter is poured into the fat and juices remaining when you have removed the beef roast to rest before carving.)

For breakfast: Set oven to 425°F. Heat a large skillet (10 to 12 inches). Swirl 2 tablespoons butter in the hot pan and immediately pour in batter. Bake for 20 minutes. You can add fruit such as apple slices and sausage slices into the pan before pouring in the batter. Serve with powdered sugar or cinnamon sugar.

EGG DISHES

OMELETTES:

I seldom make omelettes for guests as they are very last minute and quite intense. But if I have just one couple, a good omelette is really appreciated. For each person, whip 2 eggs with a bit of lemon juice, salt, and pepper. Heat an 8-inch pan over medium heat and add a slice of butter. Working quickly before the butter burns, pour in the egg mixture. Work around the pan, lifting the edge and tipping the pan so the uncooked egg flows underneath. As soon as you run out of raw egg, add a filling and fold the omelette in half as you tip it onto a plate.

Fillings: grated cheese, cream cheese, raw spinach leaves, cooked sausage, etc. You can also make a sweet omelette by adding a tablespoon of sugar to the eggs and filling with sliced fruit.

FRITTATAS:

I do love frittatas. They sit on the stove, cooking quietly while you concentrate on the rest of breakfast. Sauté some veggies such as potatoes, onions, spinach, asparagus—with some ground sausage if desired. Beat 6–10 eggs and pour over the veggies. Season with salt and pepper. Cover with grated cheese once eggs are partially set. Cover pan, keep heat on low-medium, and cook until eggs are firm. You can get decorative by adding sliced tomato wedges as the eggs set.

BREAKFAST SANDWICHES:

This is an overnight dish. All you have to do in the morning is slide it in the oven. In our family, it was the traditional Christmas morning breakfast my mother always made. It baked in the oven while we opened presents. The first sign her brain was aging was a conversation about this breakfast. She planned to bring the ingredients to our Yosemite home to prepare on Christmas Eve. She called, saying she had lost the recipe.

"No worry," I assured her. "There will be six of us for breakfast, so you'll need ingredients for six sandwiches plus a quart of milk and six eggs."

She called back, "I need 12 slices of bread, but bread isn't packaged by slices! Where do I find six eggs? Eggs are sold by the dozen! What kind of ham? Do I buy a whole ham?" Panic in her voice as her brain fails to retrieve info stored for years.

I assured her I was shopping and could pick up ingredients and help her make breakfast if she wanted. Panic subsides. Sure enough, memory returns when she makes the sandwiches. Problem solved for this Christmas. No point worrying about future holidays.

For each person:

- 2 slices white bread
- 1 slice American cheese
- 1 slice ham

Make ham and cheese sandwiches and place in a greased pan. Cover with a mixture of beaten eggs and milk (a cup of milk with two beaten eggs covers two sandwiches). Refrigerate overnight and bake at 350°F in the morning for 45 minutes.

You can make a variation using torn chunks of leftover French bread and ½ lb. grated cheese. Add cooked crumbled sausage and/or thawed frozen spinach (squeezed dry) if desired. Top with a mix of six eggs beaten with three cups of milk. Leave overnight in fridge and bake in the morning at 350°F for 45 minutes.

ROSE EGGS (SERVES 6):

These are really pretty!

- Grease or use a non-stick muffin tin.
- 12 slices black forest ham or other thin ham without holes.

Line muffin tins with ham so that the edges stick out; these will be the flower petals. Place some sautéed mushrooms in the bottom of each cup. Crack one egg into each cup. Add salt and pepper and spoon a bit of sour cream on top. Bake for 15 minutes at 350°F. (Whites should be set and yolks still runny.) Remove carefully. These are really pretty!

PEREGRINE EGGS (6 SERVINGS):

- 6 English muffins
- 6 eggs
- 1 cooked sausage, sliced crosswise
- 3 Portabello mushrooms
- Mushroom gravy

Toast muffins. For each serving, leave one half (round) and cut the other in half. The whole will be the body, the two halves the wings.

Sauté mushrooms cut in half crosswise. Starting at the curved side, slice each half into six slices, leaving the flat side intact. This will be your tail.

Poach or lightly fry 6 eggs. Place one egg on each English muffin half. Put a slice of sausage as the head. Arrange muffin halves as wings and spread mushroom slices as the tail. Cover with a bit of mushroom gravy or sour cream.

QUESADILLA PIE (4 SERVINGS):

This is a simple Mexican-inspired dish that guests love.

- 1 10-inch flour tortilla (place in a greased 8–9" pie tin)

Mix 1 cup grated cheddar cheese with a small can of chopped green chilis and ¼ cup chopped cilantro, then place on the tortilla. (You can add about 2 cups chopped rotisserie chicken to make this a dinner dish.)

Beat 2 eggs with 1 cup milk and add 1 cup flour mixed with 1 teaspoon baking powder. Pour into pie shell and top with 1 cup grated cheese.

Bake at 425–450°F for about 20 minutes. Let cool about 5 minutes before cutting into 4 wedges. Serve with salsa and sour cream.

YIN-YANG MELON SOUP:

You need two blenders and 6 white soup bowls with wide bottoms.

- Fill one blender with chopped green melon (honeydew or similar).
- Fill the second blender with chopped cantaloupe.
- Blend both until smooth.

Cut six strips of aluminum foil and fold each over three times for strength. Shape like an S to fit the bottom of the soup bowls. One person holds the foil in place while the other carefully pours the melon soups. Carefully remove the foil and you should have a green and orange yin-yang pattern.

Place a blueberry in the wide part of each shape, representing the good that is always somehow in evil, and the evil that is always somewhat present in the good.

QUICK APPETIZERS

FRIED CHEESE:

Place small piles (about 2 inches) of grated cheddar cheese on a hot, non-stick frying pan. Flip as soon as cheese starts to melt. You can also bake these in the oven at 350°F for 15–20 minutes.

SOCCA:

Popular street food in Southern France, easy to make and few people have tried it.

- 2¼ cups garbanzo flour
- 2 cups water
- 1 teaspoon salt
- 3 tablespoons olive oil (heated in a 12-inch skillet)

Pour batter into skillet and broil for 4 minutes. Shake the pan. Bake at 450°F for 6–8 minutes. Dust with black pepper.

GREEN PEA GUACAMOLE:

In a blender, place:

- 1 box frozen peas, thawed (about 1 pound)
- 2 tablespoons olive oil
- 2 tablespoons lime or lemon juice
- ¼ bunch cilantro
- ¼ cup chopped red onion
- 1 jalapeño
- ¼ tsp cumin
- ½ tsp salt

Blend and serve with tortilla chips.